HE IS KNOWN BY ONE NAME.

In Japan he learns the sacred art of the warrior.

In San Francisco, he enjoys the pleasures of the good life.

On the Mountain of Fear, he must shed the trappings of the civilized American and unleash the fearsome killing machine he was trained to be.

NINJA MASTER

Books by Wade Barker

Published by
WARNER BOOKS

NINJA MASTER

#2
MOUNTAIN
OF FEAR

Wade Barker

WARNER BOOKS

A Warner Communications Company

ACKNOWLEDGMENTS

Mr. J. B. Gross of Philadelphia, one of the few men to train with the Japanese Emperor's Guards.

Mr. Steven Hartov of New York, one of the few men to break a board, dive a sky, skin a dive, and plane a fly, all on or about his sixteenth birthday.

Mr. Christopher Browne of Wilton, Connecticut, who wouldn't know a violent act if it came up and beat him to a pulp.

And, of course, Melissa, who knew what the hell the medical term for Adam's apple was. Better living through education.

WARNER BOOKS EDITION

Warner Books, Inc., 75 Rockefeller Plaza, New York, N.Y. 10019

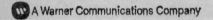 A Warner Communications Company

Printed in the United States of America

First Printing: November, 1981

10 9 8 7 6 5 4 3 2 1

DEDICATION

To Anthony F. Slez, Jr., who gets me out of trouble a lot better—and a lot more often—than he gets me in.

NINJA MASTER

#2

MOUNTAIN OF FEAR

Chapter One

The deputy put his hand inside her shirt at the same moment he pointed the gun at her face. Rosalind Cole stiffened and was about to pull back until she felt the man's stiff, calloused fingers grip her breast tighter. Using her firm chest as leverage, he pulled the woman closer to the car's window and his gun barrel. Her beautiful black face was framed in the moonlight coming over the mountain—which she could see over the deputy's right shoulder.

"Well, look what we have here," said the deputy, his hand still tight around the woman's left breast and his big revolver still pointed right at her small nose. "A nigger speeder."

Rosalind Cole wouldn't let herself become frightened. Her brain was practically screaming at the rest of her body to become petrified, but she fought the urge to get hysterical. Her dignity was about all that was left her. She couldn't pull away without causing some damage to her chest. She didn't know if she could start the Cutlass's engine and speed away before he fired the big gun of his.

There was no way to judge the policeman's character since he was just a hulking silhouette in the Virginia night.

Rosalind glanced to her right as she tried to compose herself while the cop's hand started to press and knead her flesh. Olivia Drake had pushed herself against the locked passenger door, her dark eyes wide in shock. Olivia had been the one who was reluctant to drive all night to their next shooting location. "Couldn't we hire a limo or go by train or something?" the eighteen-year-old black model had complained. "You know what they say about these Southern back roads."

Rosalind, the hotshot free-lance fashion editor, had been the one to trust in the Negro and women's liberation movements. "Come on, now, Olivia," she had impatiently complained. "You've been seeing too many episodes of 'The Dukes of Hazard.' If we're going to get this pictorial on 'The New South' done, we'll have to be in Richmond tomorrow morning. Now do you want to be on this shoot or don't you?"

Olivia had reluctantly gone along with her boss while the photographer and other models went on ahead in the company van. So it was just Rosalind and Olivia alone on the back road looking for a motel when they were pulled over by the flashing red and blue lights of a patrol car. The older woman couldn't bring herself to play the frightened innocent or the obliging nigger for the redneck cop, so she decided to put the backwoods bigot in his place.

"Can I help you, officer?" she said tougher than she felt, "or do you just want to cop a feel?"

The hand released her breast and jumped back out of the car as if stung. But the wide barrel of the shiny revolver remained motionless. Rosalind kept her gaze steady on the cop's featureless face.

"You got any kind of identification?" he drawled.

"I believe a driver's license is the customary requirement in this situation?" Rosalind replied in her best diction. She was feeling a bit more secure in the situation. He was just another dumb, horny, small-time cop out for a little nookie. At best she'd bribe him a few dollars. At worst she'd have to join him in the woods for a while. Anyway it worked, it wouldn't be anything she hadn't done before.

She saw the cop's head nod. "Get it," he instructed.

Rosalind reached over to her pocketbook, checking her outfit as she moved. Her dark suit was unrumpled by the officer's rough examination. Her white, silky shirt was still unbuttoned as far down as she always left it to expose an enticing amount of her cleavage. She grabbed her purse and looked at Olivia, who was still cowering on the other side of the seat. The editor could see sweat on the girl's round face.

"Don't worry, dear," the woman soothed, pulling the purse to her lap. Before she could snap it open, the cop reached back inside and wrenched the pocketbook out of her grasp. "Hey . . . !" she exclaimed in surprise.

"Shut up," he barked, pulling the gun barrel out of her face, but making a point of keeping it trained on her as he dumped the purse's contents out onto the hood of the Cutlass Supreme.

"Rose, they can't . . . !" Olivia blurted.

"Keep quiet, dear," Rosalind seethed through clenched teeth. "They are."

The cop threw various things aside until he came to Rosalind's billfold. He checked the wallet section and whistled at the money within. "A hundred and thirty-five dollars," he counted. He slowly pulled the money out, folded it up, and put it in his own pocket. When his hand came up again, it was holding a flashlight which he trained on the ID portion of the leather holder. He ambled back to the open window on the driver's side of the car, one hand holding the billfold and light, the other still pointing the gun.

"Hands on the dashboard," he instructed. "Keep 'em where I can see them." Both women responded slowly. Neither wanted to make the good ol' boy nervous. "You Rosalind Cole?" he asked the driver.

"That's right," the woman replied patiently. "And you are . . . ?"

"I'll ask the questions," he spat. "This don't say where you work."

"I'm a free-lance editor," Rosalind replied, not liking the direction the questions were going. "And I have a photographer waiting right now."

"So you don't work any one place?" the cop asked.

"I told you we have a photographer waiting in Richmond for us right now."

"You didn't answer my question, nigger," the cop stressed, moving closer. "You work one place?"

"No," Rosalind hastily said, her voice cracking a bit. "I work a lot of places. I'm known in a lot of places. They know me all over New York—"

The cop stopped, seemingly considering this information. Rosalind closed her eyes and prayed. The silence only made Olivia more agitated. "What's going on?" she asked in a quavering voice. "What is happening here?"

"Richmond," said the cop, leaning casually on the window of the driver's side. "New York," he drawled, the gun hanging loosely in his grip and the flashlight pointed at Rosalind's feet. Her high-heeled, strap shoes were pinioned in the portable spotlight. "Them cities is a long ways off, ladies," he continued, bringing the light up to Olivia's face. She blinked painfully in the beam, bringing her hand up to shield her eyes. "Hands on the dashboard!" the cop barked again. Reluctantly, Olivia complied, turning her head away from the light, nearly crying with fear.

"Pretty," the cop mused, moving the light from the young model's face down her body. He stared at her maroon, U-necked top tucked into her designer jeans and settled the beam on her T-strapped pumps. "Real pretty." He snapped the light up and out of the car, while straightening. "Too pretty to be speeding around the back roads without a CB in the car to let your friends know where you'll be," he said officiously. He tossed the billfold into Rosalind's lap. "Sorry about the inconvenience, ladies, but we've been having some trouble with two female bank robbers as of late. I thought you were them for sure. My mistake."

Rosalind nearly fainted with relief as the cop turned to his car and waved his gun in the air. "It's all right, Andy!" he called. He turned back to the Cutlass. "Ma'am, maybe you want to come out and collect yer stuff? Sorry I had to make such a mess."

Rosalind was so relieved that she opened the door and stepped out without question. "That's all right," she quickly replied, her relief making her talk more. "I can understand your situation." She bent to retrieve her empty pocketbook then started throwing the stuff on the hood back inside of the purse. "You can't be too careful today," she breathed hastily on. "Anybody could stab you in the back. Like my photographer and models. We've been going at it tooth and nail this whole assignment."

Rosalind heard the police car door close. She had already written off her money and forgotten about his accosting her braless chest when she realized the cop was still right behind her. The car door sound was not that of the accosting cop getting in. It was the other cop getting out.

"Oh, my God!" Rosalind gasped as she dropped her purse and ran back toward her open door. A brawny arm slammed across her chest, throwing her back to the Cutlass's hood. "Olivia, run!" she screamed before she felt a hand pull her hair and another hand push something soft, bumpy and noxious into her open mouth. Any other screams were muffled by the knotted handkerchief the cop had gagged her with.

No more screams were needed to get Olivia to move. Throughout the drive, she had played the scenario over and over in her imaginative mind. Some redneck bigots would stop them on a back road for speeding or having a taillight out or something. Then they would be railroaded into a hick jail run by a bunch of sadists who would do God knows what to them. As soon as the fantasy seemed to be coming true, Olivia had been preparing for an escape. The passenger door was open even before Rosalind had uttered her first cry. Olivia slammed one foot out onto the gravel and discovered that fashionable high heels were not good for running. That discovery saved her life.

Instead of bolting right out into the arms of the second cop, she stumbled and fell under his grip. She hit his knees with her back, throwing him even more off balance. She scrambled back to her feet as he fell and hit his temple on the edge of the open door.

Olivia took a hysterical second to check her surroundings. The nearly full moon bathed the back road in dim blue light, but between that and the double headlights of the patrol car she could see that they were on the side of a narrow two lane blacktop lined by woodland on both sides. There were just a few more yards of the abutment to go before the side of the road dipped into a dirt covered gully and the forest yawned up beyond. Olivia pushed herself in that direction.

Rosalind felt herself being bent back across the hood of her car, her screams muffled by the cloth filling her mouth. She used her arms and hands to steady herself as the pressure of the heavy cop bore down on top of her. One of his hands was still in her hair, pulling her head back, while the other was tearing at her skirt, widening its fashionable slit and pushing the hem up to her hips. Her eyes had squeezed shut with the pain, but she forced them open in time to see Olivia hobbling toward the woods and the second cop groggily rising to go after her.

Even though she saw them upside down from her position, she could see the young model would be no match for the hulking cop. She glimpsed a cut on his forehead and a curtain of blood oozing across his face, but she could also see that his features were twisted up in rage. She had to slow him down. She had already written herself off, she saw no way out for her, but she was sure Olivia could escape. Running on instinct, she slapped the sides of the hunching cop on her until she felt his gun in its holster.

It didn't occur to her to use the gun at point blank range on him and then kill the second man. She was in a state of shock which precluded her own rescue. All she could think of was getting the girl out of the predicament her boss had gotten her into. The pistol came out of the holster easily and seemed to swing up of its own volition. It stopped its arc as Rosalind's arm settled on the car hood above her head. The metal hood steadied her aim as she pulled the upside down trigger. The gun boomed and tore out of her fingers.

The .357 bullet tore into the windshield's frame and ricocheted into the second cop's upper arm. He howled in pain and the first cop looked up in surprise. In the meantime, Olivia had managed to make it to the woods. She stopped by the first tree and looked back. The cops had thrown Rosalind onto her stomach. One had pulled off her stockings and was wrapping it around her head to keep the wad of cloth in her mouth. The other was handcuffing her wrists behind her back. As soon as they had finished their quick work, the first cop spun her onto her back again and slammed the back of his hand across her face. He then pulled her down and pushed himself up so they were in a sexual position. He stopped when he noticed the second cop staring at them mutely with a smug grin on his face.

"Well, go get the other bitch," the first cop spat, slicing his arm in the forest's direction. The other cop snapped out of his voyeuristic reverie and started to turn toward the wood. Olivia didn't stay any longer. She turned away and started off in the other direction. Blindly, determinedly, she pushed her way through the trees, ignoring the lances of pain up her legs as the heels sunk into the uneven ground, twisting her thin ankles. That pain was soon joined by the jabs and cuts of branches and briars which dug into her naked arms as she ran past.

She tried to ignore it all as she moved deeper and deeper into the wood. Each succeeding obstruction seemed to loom out at her from the dim blue light like scary features inside a fun house. Deep within her subconscious, she realized how nearsighted people felt; how murky things suddenly took shape and substance right before their eyes. She ran into these things, her lips clamped down over her teeth—refusing to make a sound which would lead the psycho cops to her.

Olivia had what it took to remain silent. She had remained silent through ten years of a childhood which would make anyone scream. Then she ran away from home, getting taken in by an interracial couple in New Haven out of pure luck. They sent her to school and raised her as one of their own until her feminine beauty started to blossom at the age of fourteen. Then she took up dance and acting classes in New York. There she was noticed and started modeling for *Seventeen* magazine. One thing led to another until she found herself in a car with a fashion editor on the back roads of Virginia, just over the Pennsylvania border.

Olivia reverted back to that kid on the back streets of Boston. Pausing just a second to rip off her high heels, she kept going barefoot. She had to get to a place of safety. A tree, a cave, somewhere she could rest until she could work out a plan to get help. Until then she had to keep going . . . for Rosalind's sake. She screwed her gaze into the distance just as a horrible face loomed into view.

It was a death's head, a horribly grinning mask with blood even covering the teeth. For a split second she thought it was a hallucination brought on by shock, but then the figure below the face took shape and Olivia realized it was all too real. The figure was decked out in a cop's uniform. Olivia ran straight into it.

She looked up to see that the blood was real, oozing out of a cut on the cop's forehead. Still, the big man was grinning as if not hurt. He wrapped his arms around her little figure and lifted her right off the ground. He grasped his wrist behind her back and trapped her in a crushing bear hug. She felt her breath explode out of her mouth in a wheezing gasp, leaving her mute. She slapped both hands against his chest and pushed, but his grip didn't lessen. He pulled even tighter instead. Olivia's eyes teared and her brain was washed by a flood of sudden, pulsating colors. She sent her bare feet kicking, but it felt as if her toes were harmlessly bouncing off a cloth-covered tree trunk. She tried to bring her knee up into his crotch, but she couldn't get the leverage. She heard a dim hissing in the distance and realized it was the cop laughing.

She wrenched her misty eyes open to see his red-smeared visage stretched into an expression of vengeful humor and his forearms clenching with the effort to crush the consciousness out of her. She felt intent on smashing that look off his face but knew that she was too weak to do it. In a matter of seconds she would be knocked out. Instead she collected all the strength that was left her, bunched her fingers together and brought both fists down on the crimson-soaked hole in his sleeve.

Olivia had slammed down on the second cop's bullet wound. The man the first cop had called Andy roared his anger and dropped the girl. She didn't even wait for her breath or full vision to return to her. She landed on her feet and threw herself in the other direction—making her torso feel like some saltwater taffy which had just been snapped. Her shoulder slammed into a tree. She bounced off that and kept going. She flung one leg in front of the other as fast as she could, not knowing that all she was achieving was weaving drunkenly back and forth.

Andy caught up to her before she had gone ten yards. With his unwounded arm he slapped her on the back of the head. With a forlorn cry, Olivia fell face first onto the leaf-covered ground. Her torso smacked into something hard, sharp and unforgiving. Automatically her hands fluttered underneath her to see what it was. Just before they gripped the obstruction, Andy's hands wrapped around her elbows.

"You shouldn't 'a done that, bitch," he hissed, dropping one knee into the small of her back. "You're gonna pay for that, you nigger cunt." He released one of her elbows to wrest the pair of handcuffs from his belt. As soon as she felt her arm free, Olivia dug under her stomach to grab the rock that was between her and the soft ground. She felt the cuff wrap and click into place around one wrist. She felt Andy grab her shoulder to wrest the other arm behind her back.

She helped him out. Rather than just her arm, Olivia spun over completely, bringing the rock with her. Using it like her fist, she slugged the cop in the side of the head with it. Her arm vibrated from the force but she heard the grisly thwack of the stone crushing skin, blood, and bone. Andy didn't shout this time. He only grunted before falling heavily onto his side.

Olivia's mind was clear even before he landed. Taking no chances, she scrambled over to him, unclipped his .357 Python revolver from its holster and pulled it out. The black girl stood shakily, holding the huge weapon out in front of her in both small hands. She pointed the barrel at Andy's head and started to pull the trigger.

It was hard. She didn't know whether it was the build of the gun or her own weakness which made it so hard to get the trigger back. The revolver started vibrating and Olivia felt herself biting down on her lower lip with the effort. Then her imagination took over. She thought about the high caliber bullet tearing through the man's skin like a drill through a hunk of plaster. She envisioned his internal organs spilling out of a gaping hole in his body.

She couldn't do it. She couldn't kill him. She cursed herself, but even the thought of Rosalind getting raped back at the car couldn't bring her to a death frenzy. With a pitiful moan, she spun away from the motionless body of the second cop and kept running deeper into the forest.

The gun was like a weight attached to the end of her arm as she alternately gulped air and sobbed. She kept herself moving even when her legs felt like sacks of sand and her chest felt like the inside of a furnace. Up ahead, she saw a gleam through the trees. She pulled herself up a briar-filled incline until the fuzzy gleam became a discernible red glowing light.

It was her light at the end of the tunnel.

Olivia kept going until she had emerged from that section of the trees to the side of another road. She looked down the road in both directions. There were only two curves and more trees as far as she could see. She looked across the road at a small, rustic, wooden tavern of the type she associated with beer commercials. The red light was a neon window display which read "BUD." It was just a little bar nestled in the night along the Virginia backcountry.

In the parking lot were two cars—a van and an old soft-drink delivery truck. On the door was a sign saying "Carling Black Label—We're Open." Olivia started to cry. She had made it. She dragged herself, barely upright, across the street and fell heavily against the tavern door as she turned the knob. The heavy wooden door swung open with a bang, pulling the girl along with it.

Olivia became vaguely aware of a distinct inactivity on the other side of the door. She realized that she had blacked out for a second and was staring at the floor with her mouth agape. To her disgust, she saw that she had been drooling. She pulled her head upright, her eyes adjusted to the interior light. When she could finally see, she noted three men sitting around a table, another man looking over his shoulder behind the bar, and the white-aproned, bald bartender directly in front of her. All were staring at her. The only difference between the four other men and the bartender was that the bartender was leveling a sawed-off shotgun at her chest.

Olivia couldn't understand it for a second, then she remembered Andy's gun. She looked at it in her fingers as if it were an alien creature, then let it slip from her slick, quivering fingers. It hit the thick floor boards with a full thunk. She then pushed away from her mooring of the door and stumbled over to the bar. She landed badly, needing both hands on the bar's edge to keep her upright. She heard the clank of the handcuffs against a stool as they hung from one wrist.

"Please," she said, her voice a rusty rasp in the smoky interior of the bar. "Please." The bartender moved back from her, still keeping the shotgun aimed. She felt tears of frustration and helplessness continue out of her eyes until she caught sight of herself in the mirror behind the bar. Her entire face glowed with a fine sheen of sweat, only interrupted by lines of drooling red where she had been cut. Her lips were full and red but the red dribbled off her bottom lip and across her chin where she had bitten it. Her curly mane of dark hair was flecked with twigs and leaves. Her arms were shiny and cut and her shirt was torn open in several revealing places.

Olivia tore her eyes off her own reflection and looked toward the others for help. "Please," she repeated hoarsely to the trio of seated men, "my friend . . . my friend and I were at . . . at . . . attacked." She could hardly hear her own voice so she wasn't sure the men had gotten the message. She gulped air desperately, trying to get enough strength to deliver her plea in full cry.

"Call the sheriff, Mel," the bartender told one of the sitting men.

"No!" Olivia shouted, spinning to the bartender. He stepped back again and pushed the gun forward. "No," Olivia repeated with more control. "My friend, Rosalind, and I were attacked. Just across the way. You must help!"

"Then you'll be wantin' the sheriff, Missy," the bartender said carefully. "Call him, Mel." The three men started to get up.

"No!" Olivia cried again. She strived for a coherent way of getting her plight across. "Don't you understand? We were attacked by two men in police uniforms. In a police car! They must've disguised themselves and stolen the car somehow. Don't you see? You've got to help me now, yourselves!"

"You're safe now, Missy," said one of the men. "Don't worry. If those men are fakes, the sheriff'll know it." All three men were on their feet and moving around the table.

"Rosalind is still out there!" Olivia exploded. "We've got to save her now. We can't wait for the sheriff!"

"Nothing we can do," soothed one of the other men. "If they do have your friend, they're probably long gone by now. There's nothing we can do to stop them."

Olivia's mind was in a turmoil. She was sure the cops who stopped her weren't fakes but she couldn't tell these men that. She thought and looked around for some way out. The bald, brawny, overweight bartender kept the shotgun trained on her. One of the men eased over toward the revolver she had dropped as the other pair approached her.

The black girl tried bolting from the stool to retrieve the gun before they got it, but the two men caught her between them like practiced warders. Their arms simply made a human net which Olivia fell into. Once stopped, the four hands pinioned her arms and wrapped around her chin. In seconds, she was immobilized.

"There, there," one of the men cooed as they drew her back to the bar. She writhed in their grip, locking gazes with the fifth man in the room—an innocuous, sandy-haired man in the corner of the bar with a socket wrench in his hand. His gaze seemed to go right through her, his face empty of any expression. Somehow, he, more than anyone else in the room, frightened her.

The men holding her seemed to notice the man at the same time. For his benefit they started a little show which served to tighten a noose around Olivia's neck. First the third man from the table picked up the revolver. "A .357 Python," he said. "Just like the kind the deputies use."

Olivia moaned in horror as she realized what they were trying to do. In answer to her exclamation, one of the men wrenched her arm up behind her back in a terribly painful hold. Another arm tightened around her neck, making breathing difficult.

"Looks like the deputy's cuffs, too," commented one of her captives, fingering the bracelet of steel around one wrist.

Even through the pain and the crushing hold, Olivia managed to contest their findings. She bucked and grunted "no, no, no. . . ." This time one of the men pulled her other arm up her back and clicked the free cuff in place. Her hands were locked behind her. Then, with his free limb, he shoved his hand over her mouth. What sounds were able to get past the forearm around her neck, bubbled incoherently against the fingers pressed against her lips.

"Damn jail," the bartender muttered. He lowered the

shotgun and moved toward the sandy-haired fifth man. "Those damn cells are antique," he said for the man's benefit. "Any school chile could get out of one. Would you believe this is the second jailbird we had come stumblin' in here this week?" Keeping up his muttering, the bartender gave the gun to the sandy-haired guy, ducked under the bar opening, and moved for the phone himself. "Give the boys a hand while I call the sheriff, would ya?" he said over his shoulder. "Just keep her covered, huh?"

Everyone seemed to pause as the fifth man looked at the gun in his hand. The man holding the revolver tightened his grip on the trigger and prepared himself to use the gun if the stranger said or did anything but what he was told. But finally the sandy-haired guy brought the shotgun to bear on the girl's head. The girl stared at him pleadingly.

"Fine," he said unemotionally. "The nigger gal'll get what she deserves."

Olivia closed her eyes and nearly fainted with despair. The men smiled as the bartender dug into his pocket for a dime. Just then the door swung open again and Andy came roaring into the bar.

"Goddamm it!" he exploded, swinging his head this way and that. "Any of you fellers see a nigger gal go hightailing here . . . ?" He stopped when he saw Olivia struggling in the men's grip. A big, vengeful smile appeared on the cop's face as he moved forward, but then he saw the stranger behind the bar. The man had the shotgun now trained on Andy's chest. "Who's that?" the cop demanded of the bartender.

"Just a good, old-fashioned businessman," the bartender said expansively, clapping Andy on the shoulder. "He just come in here earlier tonight and offered me a soda service at a price I couldn't refuse. He was ready, willin' and able to install it, so I figgered 'what the hell.' "

"Looks like the filly gave you some trouble," the man with the shotgun said, motioning toward Andy's various wounds.

"Yeah," the cop remembered, swinging his attention

back to Olivia. "Fucking little cow. . . ." He moved toward her ominously, his fists clenching and unclenching.

"Now just hold on a minute, Andy," the bartender exclaimed, pushing him back. "You're in no shape to take this nigger gal into custody. You just set down here and let us take care of everything."

"Yeah, that's right," said the man holding the revolver. "Let us take the filly into the sheriff. Three against one is better than one against one, 'specially in the shape you're in."

The bartender got Andy to a stool as the men kept Olivia still between them. The cop stared at the girl bucking in the men's grip and then started smiling again. "All right," he said faintly. "All right, he repeated, now louder and with more conviction, "but you guys make sure she gets to the sheriff's office, you hear?"

"Don't fret," one of the men said leeringly, looking down at the tight black package. "She'll be waiting for you when you get back from the doc."

"Okay, so it's settled then," said the bartender. He came back toward the bar and flipped the man with the shotgun a dime. "Call Doc Carver while I get this hardworking deputy a brew." He winked at Andy. "For medicinal purposes, a'course."

The sandy-haired man threw the shotgun back to the barkeep while catching the dime nimbly in his other hand. The bartender caught the weapon in return and clapped the sandy-haired man on the shoulder as he passed. The man went for the phone as the trio dragged the sobbing girl out.

"Look at this nigger, would ya?" one of the men said. Just look at her." The man at the phone noticed that the guy was grinding her ample breast with one hand.

"I wouldn't mind a taste of that," said the sandy-haired man.

"Well, come on down to the sheriff's office when you're through here, boy," said the breast grinder. "But don't rush. We'll be making the trip nice and slow." With that, the men had gotten the girl out the door.

The sandy-haired man took the phone off the hook and brought the dime up to the slot. Even if Andy had been standing right next to him and staring at the ten-cent slot, he wouldn't have been able to tell that the man palmed the dime just as it seemed the coin would go in. The man dialed information and asked for Carver's number. He hung up and coughed to cover the fact that there was no coin return. He palmed the same coin again when "calling" the doc. Finally he hung up and went back toward the bar.

"So," Andy was saying, "after the cunt gets ahold of my gun and lets me have it in the arm, she bashes me on the head. Some little bitch, huh?"

"Yeah," said the bartender. "But she was some good-lookin' gal for a nigger, wasn't she?"

The sandy-haired man made an elaborate show of sitting down next to the deputy while pocketing the palmed dime. "It's all set," he said. "The doc'll see you any time you're ready."

"Great," said the bartender. "How about a brew?"

"Well, actually," the stranger drawled, "I could use a Coke. My stuff is all hooked up, so why don't you give it a try?"

"Great," the barkeep repeated, pulling out an empty glass and moving toward the spigot at the end of the bar.

"Put some ice into it," the sandy-haired man suggested. "I like a lot of ice." Then he grinned.

"Sure," said the bartender, scooping up some cubes. He pressed one of the buttons on the bulbous plastic nozzle connected to a hose which sunk into a tank on the floor and a stream of dark, carbonated liquid spurted out. "Hey, it works fine," added the bartender, bringing the foaming soda over.

"Yeah, but here's the true test," said the stranger, taking the glass and bringing it up to his lips. The two other men watched as the stranger completely drained the glass with one long pull. The man put the glass down in triumph. "Perfect," he said.

"Yeah, well," said deputy Andy. "I've got to get going." He took a last gulp of the beer in front of him. "Thanks,

Stan," he said to the bartender, not noticing the sandy-haired man digging a square ice cube out of his empty glass and keeping it in the palm of his left hand. "I'll be in touch."

Before the cop could even get off his stool, however, the stranger spoke up. "But what's your hurry, Andy?" the sandy-haired man asked. "Don't you remember? That nigger gal done killed you when she slugged your head."

If the two men had any sense at all, they would've gone for their guns. Instead they watched in amazement as the sandy-haired stranger crushed the ice cube in his left hand. Then they saw a blurred movement. That was the last thing they ever saw.

Although the stranger made no noise there seemed to be an explosion of sound inside the bar as a mass of air was violently displaced by the stranger's sharp, stunning thrust. His left hand moved straight forward, the palm out, shards of broken ice pointed at the bartender like glass blades. His right hand propelled the bottom of the soda glass unerringly toward the rock wound on the deputy's left temple. Both makeshift weapons hit at the same time.

The stranger's blows were so perfect and so devastating that Andy's temple was crushed—blood spurting out his ear as he slid completely off the stool. Neither the glass broke or the stool tipped. The ice shards dug right through Stan's skin and into arteries carrying nutriment to his brain. By the time the bartender's head flew back, the sandy-haired man's hands were already back at his side.

If a witness had blinked, he would have missed the blows. If a witness had blinked, all he would have seen were two men fall lazily down, dead before they hit the floor. But there was no witness. There was only Brett Wallace to survey his own handiwork.

He felt miraculously calm for a man who had just killed two others. As always since his return from the Orient, he had reached an entirely alien realm of calm before he had to deliver killing blows. He did not consider the various humanistic aspects of what he had just done. He merely thought about his goal and the method with which to achieve it. He quickly looked over the room. He did not bother checking the men. He already knew they were dead. If anything had gone wrong, his body would have told him even before his blows were completed.

He noted the ice cubes from his glass across the bar top. In minutes they would be puddles of water and by the end of the hot night dry up completely. He noted the simple soda machine in the corner. He would have to dismantle it and get it back in the truck before the bodies were discovered. He couldn't risk having anything to link him to the deaths here. With the soda machine and his truck gone, the sheriff could only assume that the girl had killed all the men.

Wallace went ahead to complete that image. First he picked up the bartender's shotgun and emptied the barrels point blank into the already dead bodies. Then he went out into the night to find and eliminate three more men who knew of his existence.

The good old boys were taking it nice and slow. Their van slowly weaved back and forth across the tree-lined road at a maximum speed of twenty-five-miles-per-hour. It had to go that slow so the three men could take turns leaping from the driver's seat to the naked, bound, black-skinned bundle in the rear of the vehicle. The only sound to disturb the darkness was the laughter of the men and the sobbing of the girl.

Olivia had long since spit out the socks that the trio had stuffed into her mouth, but the thin leather belt that was supposed to hold them there was still taut between her teeth. Her bloody hands, her long, painted fingernails now chipped and broken, were still in the handcuffs. Her clothes had been cut and tugged off her body. The men, too, were mostly naked. They took turns on various areas of her body as the van turned corners, went down inclines, struggled up hills, and took curves.

The van was a simple affair. Two doors in the front like any car and then two doors that swung out on the back side. The windows on the back doors were spray-painted opaque. Olivia was too low to see out the front windshield or for anybody outside to see her. She just continued to struggle in hot, numb terror.

The man known as Mel left her frenzied warmth to take over the wheel. He started to turn a corner, then looked back as his pals teamed up to give themselves pleasure, one was working the front and one was working the rear. Mel laughed and looked back at the road in time to avoid hitting an old soda fountain truck that was parked horizontally across both lanes.

He jammed on the brakes, jerking his passengers forward even at their slow speed. He heard the girl cry out in pain before the others started complaining. Mel didn't answer them at first, just stared at the soda truck strangely. There was something familiar and ominous about its presence there. Mel couldn't put his finger on it, but for some reason the automotive barrier sobered him up immediately.

"Give me Andy's gun," he shouted to the men in the back without turning around. Instead he scanned both sides of the road for any sign of life.

"What the hell is it?" asked one of the other men, using Olivia's body as a leverage to sit up. "What d'ya want it for?"

Still without turning around, Mel shoved his hand at the men and wiggled his fingers in a demanding motion. "Nothing," he said, "just give it to me, will ya?"

The other man reached across Olivia's body and pulled the heavy revolver off a makeshift shelf on the van panel —too high for the girl to reach it. He slapped it into Mel's waiting hand. "If it's nothing, what do you need the gun for?" he asked.

Mel checked the chamber. A shell was in each. He clicked it shut, the noise seeming to echo in the van. "There's a disabled truck blocking the road, that's all," he told the men, looking at them this time. "I just want to make sure no out-of-towners get a look at our cargo. You keep her quiet, y'hear?" He waved the gun barrel at the bound girl, who responded by trying to scream past the belt between her teeth.

The other two men fell upon her. They practically broke a few fingers in their haste to close her mouth. "Here, here," said one, reaching into a duffel bag on the passenger's seat. He pulled out a long, wicked Bowie hunting knife. He put the flat of his hand against her chest to keep her down and the edge of the blade against her neck. "This'll keep her mouth shut." Then he planted a wet, sloppy kiss on the bottom of her face.

Mel nodded with a smile, raised the revolver, opened the driver's door, and got out. He stood on the asphalt road just before it reached a sloping incline. The blacktop curved to the left to disappear behind some trees after the top of this hill—upon which the soda truck rested. Mel moved to the front of his van. He looked both ways, but all he could see were trees bathed in the deep blue of moonlight. He listened carefully, but all he could hear were the night sounds of birds and insects. He moved closer to the blocking truck.

As he approached, he realized why it looked so familiar. It was the same truck that had been parked at Stan's tavern. It was the vehicle the sandy-haired stranger had been using. Then, on the driver's window, he saw a telltale orange sticker indicating a disabled car. That relaxed him completely. The guy must've been in such a hurry to get to the sheriff's office that his truck couldn't take it. It just died right in the middle of a turn.

Mel looked all around for any sign of the stranger. He could see nothing. It was too bad, he thought. If the guy had only stayed by his truck he could've partaken of a little dark meat. Almost as soon as Mel had that thought, he heard a dim whistling sound to his left.

At first he thought it was a bird, but the high, quiet tone was too consistent for an animal to make. He looked at the tires of the truck and van to see if any were leaking and flat, but they all looked solid. Then he tried to pinpoint the direction the sound was coming in. He took a few steps toward the woods to his left. The whistling got slightly

28

louder, but all he could see were blue trees. Then he realized that a section of the blue trees seemed blurred—as if he were looking at them through water.

Something suddenly grabbed his attention and riveted him to the spot. To the right of the blurred trees were two eyes. Just two eyes. They were hanging in the air almost six feet off the road. Mel blinked, believing he must be more tired and drunk than he had thought earlier. But when he looked again the eyes were still there. Next he thought they must be the eyes of some owl off in the trees. But then he noticed that these eyes were steel gray and human shaped. In fact, they were the size of a man's eyes not ten feet from him.

His mouth opened, but only the confused sound of "What?" came out. He stared a second more as the whistling sound moved up and off the musical scale to become a burning hum. Then, from just below the gray eyes came the sound of words.

"I came for my taste," the flat, even voice said.

Then, before Mel could even bring the .357 up, Brett Wallace sent the weighted end of his *kyotetsu-shoge* into the side of Mel's head. The specially reinforced elastic cord attached to the small, rounded weight responded beautifully, seemingly going right through the head before returning unerringly to Brett's grip. The only sound was the vicious whirring and a small, liquid smack when the weight hit, and then the night was quiet again.

The rapist's head had snapped not quite to the front and not quite to the side before he merely fell forward from a standing position, both arms at his side. It almost looked like a joke the way Mel was standing one second, then falling forward the next. The revolver didn't even clatter on the ground since it never left his grip. Brett walked soundlessly over to the body, preparing the *kyotetsu-shoge* for his next throw. It was a very simple affair consisting of a length of special cord with a weight on one end and a two-edged blade on the other. The whole implement was colored in such a way that when spun it all but disappeared.

Brett reached down, not even seeing his hand, to grab the .357. He too was colored in such a way that he seemed to be invisible. He was wearing the time tested uniform of the ninja. Almost every inch of him was covered with a dark blue cloth which blended him in with the night. The only space was a slit in the hood for his eyes. Brett, as always, had darkened his lids so with his eyes closed, there was nothing to reveal the camouflage. He had walked out from the wood and approached Mel precisely with his eyes closed—finding his target with his other five senses.

Rising to his full five-eleven height between the front of the van and Mel's motionless body, Brett quickly re-examined the situation. Mel's head was still intact, although he might already be dead. But for appearances sake, it had to appear that he was killed by Olivia with Andy's gun. There was no way the sheriff could believe that a little black girl, even a terrorized one, would have the strength to splatter Mel's brains all over the place.

Brett looked to the van's windshield. As he expected, the other two men hadn't bothered to back Mel up. They were too lust-crazed and Olivia was too beautiful to waste any of the trip to the sheriff. Besides, Brett had killed the first rapist within a minute of his leaving the vehicle. Now all he had to do was get rid of the other two without them harming the girl.

Bret walked boldly to the front of the van. He looked into the back through the windshield. Even if the others had been looking back they might not have seen him, but as it was they had all their attention on the girl. Even with a knife against her throat, Brett saw, they weren't delaying their vicious advances. One man was smiling down at her tear-stained face while massaging her chest. The other—his back to Brett—was grinding his hips between her legs while holding the knife none too steadily.

For a split second Brett's consciousness was hurled back almost fifteen years. He saw, in his mind's eye, another scene of horror and degradation. He remembered a young, dark-haired man coming back to his parent's party after giving a friend a ride home to find his folks and Oriental wife brutally murdered and debased. He recalled the scene with almost crystal clarity. His mind did not have to embellish the horrible details at all. The stink was still in his nostrils, the crimson-splashed vision was still burned into his retina, and a rending scream would always stay in his memory.

The man who had experienced that was the same man who stood in front of the van on this hot Virginia night. But it was not the same person. This person felt no horror at the scene. This man didn't rage in empathy or pity with the girl's plight. This man didn't even sweat. This man knew that he would save her. But he also knew that he could not have done it before now. She had to suffer a bit to prevent her permanent suffering. If Brett had attempted any rescue before this, it would have been only worse for the both of them.

The ninja master moved several steps back, raised the revolver, pointed it precisely at the van's windshield and pulled the trigger six times with seemingly no effort.

The high-caliber bullets—fired at point blank range—demolished the windshield. It exploded inward in a hail of spinning shards, the lead projectiles tearing out the back door above the heads of the two men.

Brett didn't want to splatter the rapists here because he couldn't afford to have bloodstains all over the road. He didn't have time to mop that mess up and it would be more logical for Olivia to have gotten Andy's gun and wasted everyone at the tavern. But mercy was the last thing on Brett's mind. The two remaining men reacted exactly as Brett expected they would. He heard the shouts and the rear doors flying open even as he ran toward the van front.

With a simple jump, Brett was on the roof of the van and moving quickly toward the back even as his *kyotetsu-shoge* was unfurled and whirring again. One man was still holding Olivia with the knife against her throat. He did not hear Brett on the roof nor did he feel the van rocking with the weight of the ninja's steps. All he saw was his friend scramble out the back doors which he had kicked open.

He didn't see Brett standing at the very back of the van's roof, whirling his ninja weapon, and neither did the man jumping to his feet outside. All Olivia's attacker saw was his friend suddenly rear back and fall as if slugged by an invisible Clint Eastwood.

"Ted?" he called, pushing the blade tighter against the girl's throat in panic. "Ted?" His only answer was the appearance of a shape that looked like an upside-down head at the top of the door opening. Suddenly, in the middle of the shape, two eyes appeared staring at him. Then an arm seemed to grow out of the side of the head.

Olivia's attacker felt the urge to drive the knife into the girl's throat. With her gone, the sheriff would back him up, and there would be no one to say they had done wrong. The man felt his muscles bunch as sweat instantly appeared on his forehead, but he didn't feel his knife hand going anywhere. He looked down in shock. A thin cord had wrapped itself completely around his hand. He looked back up at the head shape. It was gone. Instead the cord seemed to shoot out into the night and disappear into nothingness.

But suddenly that taut nothingness pulled and the man followed the pull as he fell off the girl, over the van floor, and out into the road. He lost the knife when he hit the blacktop. He rolled, twisted, and tried to get up. Halfway there, he found himself staring directly into two steel gray eyes. He opened his mouth to scream. What felt like four little rocks sunk into his neck. Any sound he tried to make was trapped in his chest. He felt like he was drowning and then he fell into a bottomless unconsciousness. He would fall with a soundless scream and never wake up.

Olivia Drake had long since stopped feeling pain. She lay numb, feeling the dead weight of her sleeping, hand-cuffed arms, and the constant ache of her leather-gagged mouth. She was alternately chilled by her own cold sweat and dried by the humid summer air. Suddenly she felt the belt leave her mouth. Seconds later she felt a tingly liquid across her face. It reminded her that she was thirsty. She made little noises and gulped as if to drink. She heard a soft, sympathetic voice.

"It's carbonated water. Take it slow."

She felt a warm hand tilt her chin and the bubbly liquid slowly coursed into her mouth. She drank gratefully. Her vision cleared somewhat and she looked up into the face of the sandy-haired stranger who had been at the tavern. He had pulled back a hood and was dressed in dark blue. His outline was a little more discernible inside the van, but still he often seemed to be nothing more than a floating head. Only this time the face that had frightened her so much at the tavern filled her with hope and faith. A little of her ghetto-survivor spirit returned to her.

"What—what took you so long?" she asked after he had finished pouring. She barked a sad excuse for a laugh.

Brett stretched his lips into something that wasn't quite a grin. "It would have been too messy back there," he said. He left it at that. He didn't have time to explain.

"My arms!" Olivia moaned, indicating some feeling was returning to her.

Brett didn't reply. He merely moved his fingers in front of the girl's face and a small, dark metal toothpick seemed to materialize in his hand. He turned her over gently—as if she were light as a feather. A few seconds later the metal bonds fell away.

Olivia pulled her arms painfully out in front of her and used the man's left arm as a rope to climb up into a sitting position. As she did so, she pulled up his dark blue sleeve by accident. Getting to her haunches she saw a thin, white scar on his pale beige forearm. She looked from that into his face.

"Who?" she asked. "What are you?"

Without a hint of humor, he replied flatly. "I am no one."

Chapter Two

Two years ago, Brett Wallace heard the *shuriken* before he saw it. And he saw it just a split second before it sunk into his left forearm which he had instinctively raised to a blocking position. If his arm had not stopped it, the five-pointed metal star would have sunk into his forehead.

He had been approaching the door of his Sausalito, California, house on a Tuesday morning after his busy three day weekend of socializing when it happened. As usual, he had dined at the Alta Mira overlooking the San Francisco Bay for Sunday brunch. That evening he took a beautiful companion, Lynn McDonald, out to a performance of the San Francisco Live Theater before having some drinks at the Trident—a waterfront watering hole, where the lights of the small boats and the city glisten across the bay's surface.

He stayed the evening with Lynn, cooking her a special feast in the morning which they shared. They spent that day together as well, stopping off at 221 Baker Street, a restaurant at the top of the Holiday Inn, for lunch. As usual, he washed down his food with liberal portions of Absolut vodka, his favorite beverage.

That evening, as every Monday night, he took advantage of his standing reservation at his favorite small French restaurant just off Clement near 10th. Lynn and he ate there before returning to her condo for another evening of lovemaking. Brett considered it a joyful couple of days— and not unusual ones. In the short time Brett had lived in Sausalito, he had made ample use of its social facilities, meeting and dating some of the city's most beautiful women. He attracted them with his poise, assurance, and dazzling talents. He was as good in the kitchen as he was in the bedroom.

He always ground his own coffee beans and added spice and fruit peels to enhance the flavor. He would always follow his after-dinner coffee with a glass of fine brandy. And his home-cooked dinners always consisted of something exotic which he would prepare precisely and indulge in with gusto. He approached sex in the same way. The preparation was precise and the act was glorious. He reveled in his ability to give his partners pleasure. Only occasionally did the image of his raped and murdered wife swim into his vision. And when it did, he would drive it away with the skill of his sexual technique.

He had continued in his hedonistic patterns, desperately enjoying life, until the moment the *shuriken* had sunk into his forearm.

All the skills he had learned in the twenty-eight years he had been studying the martial arts came to bear. The nine years he had studied the art of the ninja in Japan with Master Yamaguchi came to the forefront as he ignored the pain and prepared to face his assailant.

He heard another noise coming from his left, so he pulled the star out of his arm and threw it at the sound as he vaulted the stairway to his front door. He did not land in his front yard as he assumed he would. Instead he collided with a grate of bamboo poles, mounted a foot off the ground in such a way that the spaces between them were just not enough to get a human foot through. If Brett had landed heavily, he would have broken a few toes. Instead, he just managed to hurl himself off the trap, twist in the air and land on his feet.

He could tell from a glance that the poles were reinforced with metal bars inside them. With one swipe, he cut one such pole from the others and brought it up to serve as a *jo*—a long staff. He held it in his right hand, letting his injured left arm hover around his torso as a second defense. He heard more noises, now coming from his right. He whirled in that direction just in time to deflect an arrow from sinking into his neck with the pole.

He deflected another from his chest with a quick sideways swipe, then another from his stomach with a downward jab, then another from his pelvis with a quick upward thrust. Finally he heard no more arrows coming. But just as he relaxed, a final arrow ripped into the bamboo staff itself and tore it out of Brett's hand.

The Occidental now knew what he was dealing with, even as he fell and rolled toward cover. This was not just a bunch of hoodlums or professional hit men after him; this was a martial arts expert—an expert in the very things Brett had been trained in. And he already had Brett at a disadvantage. The American had been taken by surprise and wounded.

Brett rolled to his feet behind a tree. As he rose he caught a glimpse of a shadowy figure dressed in black coming around the side of the tree. He swung his right hand in a vicious *tsuki-waza*—a direct strike of the arm in the Shotokan style of karate. To his surprise, Brett's side-hand blow went right through the approaching clothes and sunk into the tree trunk behind them. Brett had not been prepared to strike the tree so a momentary lance of pain jabbed his upper arm. Even as he was adjusting to this surprise, a sharp, hard weight smashed across his shoulders.

Brett flew forward, vaguely aware that he had been tricked. The dark clothes had been merely that; dark clothes set on a scarecrow figure that loomed up at him out of the dark. His real assailant had been up in the tree. Once Brett had exposed himself by striking the diversion, the antagonist merely hit him with a two-legged kick. Brett slapped his hand on the ground as he flew over it, twisted in midair and reached for the *shuriken* on his own belt buckle, where he always kept it.

He landed on his feet to find it wasn't there. As soon as he made that discovery he heard another sound and saw the belt the *shuriken* had been attached to fall away from his pants. He looked up to get his first decent look at his assailant. The man was dressed in the classical guise of the ninja. He was covered head to foot in basic black with a cap, face mask, tights, rubber-soled shoes, loose blouse, and sash. In the sash was a *zutsu,* a scabbard. In his hand was a *wakizashi,* the short samurai sword.

Brett took up a position of defense. The attacking ninja didn't move. He stood with the sword outstretched and his other hand inside his blouse as if he were a statue. Brett moved forward threateningly. The ninja did not move. The small figure looked like an extremely threatening lawn jockey. Brett, for the first time in a decade, began to sweat with fear. He realized he could do one of two things. He could try to retreat or he could attack. Either way, the American wasn't sure he would succeed. He had already proven himself unprepared, incorrect, and easily fooled. On top of his fear, Brett felt shame.

He faced his assailant, forcing himself to be as motionless. The two men faced each other at three-thirty in the morning on Brett Wallace's dark lawn, waiting to see what would happen. They stood that way for a half hour, the only noticeable motion being the wind through Brett's sandy hair and the blood oozing from his arm wound. Finally it was the weakness of his digestion that forced the match to continue. All the beer, vodka, coffee, and brandy Brett had imbibed tried to smash its way out of his bladder. He was forced to act or shame himself even further.

He moved forward, preparing himself to deflect the

frighteningly sharp *wakizashi* blade while delivering a crippling blow with his injured left arm. Brett put the action into effect perfectly; and had the sword still been where he was chopping it would have worked. Only neither the sword nor the ninja was where Brett was fighting. The assailant had slipped under Brett's attack, pausing only to whip his hand out of his blouse and hurl a cloud of dust into Brett's face.

The dirt sunk into Brett's open eyes and seemed to sting his entire head. For a second he couldn't prevent his hands from leaving their defensive position and trying to scrape the pain from his head, but a moment later he had forced himself back into a pose of blind readiness. It was all in vain. The unmistakable sound of ninja cord being hurled cut through the night and wrapped itself around his body, pinning his arms to his side. But there was still the *keri-waza;* the attack with his feet and legs.

Brett flailed the air with vicious kicks, trying to protect himself and pinpoint his attacker's position. But everywhere he turned, the ninja slipped through his defenses and pelted him with numbing blows. Finally Brett felt fingers of steel dig into the side of his neck causing a pain he had never before experienced. This paralyzing pain was soon replaced by a strange tingling and he felt his entire body go blank. He wondered if this was what death felt like.

It was not death. It was close, but not quite. Brett Wallace awoke amid a small puddle of his own waste. He was lying in his own living room. The smell was much worse than it should have been. When Brett sat up and looked around, he realized why. The morning sun streaming in his windows illuminated the carnage around him. Initially it looked as if the house had been ransacked but nothing was taken. But on closer examination it became clear that the only things strewn around him were the contents of his kitchen, bathroom, and bar.

All his booze was spilled out of broken bottles. Mounds of coffee beans stained the carpet. Raw, spoiling meat had been thrown everywhere. Something vicious, enraged, and powerful had swept through his home.

As soon as Brett realized this, something else entered his vision. Up until that moment he realized that he had been looking almost right at him but hadn't seen him. Sitting not ten feet away from him on top of Brett's living room bar was Master Yamaguchi. He was wearing the same outfit he had on several hours before, with the short samurai sword still in his hand, only the cap and mask had been pulled off.

"Teacher. . . ." Brett exclaimed.

"Say nothing," Yamaguchi said quietly, his dark eyes riveting Wallace as effectively as his ropes had done. "Save for the answers to my questions. Do you know why I am here?"

Brett took in the devastation around him with his peripheral vision, keeping his gaze locked to his master's. When the memory of how badly he had been beaten returned to him, he couldn't help looking away.

"To kill me," Brett said with renewed shame.

"No," Yamaguchi intoned. "You gave your life up to us a decade ago when it had been shattered by the deaths of your family and your brutal killings of the murderers. You came to me and asked to be trained as a ninja warrior. To learn the art of stealth and know what it truly means to be an avenging shadow. You took my teachings toward a purpose: a purpose to help others as wronged as you, yourself, were.

"But soon I discover that you have taken all I had taught you in ten years and turned it against yourself. You ingest materials that cripple the pure functions of your body. You waste your skills in meaningless sexual liaisons which only serve to point out how empty your life has become. And what is worst, you actively seek an existence of attention, continually thrusting yourself into the limelight as a businessman and status seeker. You are seen everywhere in the company of the most attractive and noticeable women. You flaunt your expertise in the arcane arts as if it were some sort of hobby. You take friends into your confidence as if ninja training was some sort of remedial summer course!

"This is not the way of the ninja!" Yamaguchi exploded, fairly vibrating in rage.

"Master, please," Brett almost begged from his position on the floor. "If you must kill me, do so. Do not shame yourself with mercy because of our friendship."

"No," said Yamaguchi again, calm and motionless once more atop the bar. "Our friendship only makes my pain for you all the more intense. I have not come to kill you, my friend. I have come to ask why you are trying to kill yourself."

Brett was not ashamed to remember it. He recalled that he had cried for several hours after that. He had incoherently poured out all the pain and meaninglessness of his existence without his dead wife, Kyoko. When she and his beloved parents were murdered, he had unknowingly set his own feet on a road to hell. He had become a ninja warrior to destroy whatever he saw as evil while never admitting that the one he most wanted to see put out of his misery was himself. Subconsciously he sought the greatest danger in the hopes of having a stronger opponent kill him with honor.

All this had come out after his arm had been attended to and the two men—teacher and student—were on a plane back to Japan where the education process would start all over again.

"The ninja are not afraid of death," Yamaguchi informed him, "but nor do they seek it. The true philosopher understands death but does not follow it. And the true philosopher knows that one does not see something as evil. Evil is. Evil exists. One knows evil, one does not see it."

Brett Wallace relearned the truths of the way he had chosen for himself. Once they had landed in Tokyo, they traveled by train to Chiba, the location of one of but two ninja schools left in the world. The other, in Hokuriku, was where Brett first learned the craft. This time, in Chiba, he was reintroduced to his second teacher, Master Torii.

"So, Brett-san," the little man decked out in the outfit of a Shoalin monk said. "You have not yet succeeded in your quest for self-annihilation."

"No, Teacher," he replied, executing the customary salute—a hand held up perpendicular to the center of the chest—and bow. "I shall no longer seek the coward's road."

Torii smiled and beckoned Brett to join him on a walk around the temple's garden. The Chiba training ground was similar to the Hokuriku's location, since both were self-contained villages surrounded by walls with a temple and castle serving as a centerpiece. The gardens were beautiful, as ever, and walking amid them brought Brett a peace he was never able to attain anywhere else.

"I was certain your many women would be your destruction," Torii told him as they walked slowly. "They cannot keep their tongues still even after you cut them out. Lying on the ground, outside their mouths . . . still it is flap, flap, flap." The little master made the motion of a fish out of water with his hand.

"I shall only put faith in Rhea Tagashi," Brett assured him. "The one you sent me to a year ago."

"A fine woman," Torii admitted, "for a woman. She runs the San Francisco restaurant you co-own, is that not right?"

"The 'Rhea Dawn,' " Brett named. "Yes."

"You will sign ownership over to her completely upon your return," Torii instructed. "A ninja is a shadow warrior. *Kagemusha.* He is not the owner of a restaurant." The little master said the last sentence with almost infinite disgust. "Carry on your life with Tagashi as before," he continued, "but no longer eat among outsiders. You are not to be seen. You are to let others see you."

"Yes, Teacher," Brett replied.

"Now this other," said Torii with concern. "This Jeff Archer . . . ?"

"The young man who runs my dojo in San Francisco," the American explained.

"Incredible!" Torii exploded. "A ninja who announces

to the world that he is a master of martial arts? Unthinkable! You must renounce ownership of this martial arts studio immediately!"

"You mean, close it down?"

If Torii had any hair, he might have started ripping it out. As it was, it looked like he was hard pressed not to tear out Brett's. "Have you learned nothing? A ninja's greatest weapon is his invisibility. A ninja does nothing to call attention to himself. A ninja never swaggers, a ninja never gives a show of force before striking. To close the dojo would only attract attention, *hai?* No, you must make it clear to Archer-san that he owns and runs the studio alone."

Torii stopped and fixed Brett with a strong gaze. "Have you been teaching this young man? Have you imbued into him your self-destructive ways?"

Brett considered the master's question seriously. Torii's outburst before had not worried him. He knew that master ninjas only showed emotion when they wanted to. Torii's exclamations were only used for dramatic effect. But these last questions were asked in deadly earnest. "I may have, Teacher. Hopefully the young man is wiser than I have been."

"You must see if you can trust this man, Brett-san," Torii warned. "If you can reeducate him he can become *genin*—an agent—to your *jonin* and Tagashi's *chunin*." Jonin meant the ninja leader while the chunin was the subleader.

"He has the skill," Brett assured him.

"He must have the soul," Torii countered. "The soul that is dark but still light. The darkness of death and the light of hope. You must teach him that your arts are not games to be trifled with. You are not entering a class . . . you are embarking on a life where there is no turning back."

"And if he cannot acquire the soul?" Brett asked, already knowing the answer.

"Then you must kill him," Torii replied effortlessly and

with absolutely no dramatic effect. It was not meant as a shock or a threat. It was a statement of fact.

Brett Wallace's life began again for the third time. He had died once when his wife and family were murdered. He had died a second time when Yamaguchi had hurled the shuriken into his arm. This was his final life. It is as the haiku—with which Ian Fleming titled one of his last James Bond books—said:

> "You only live twice,
> once when you are born,
> and once when you look death in the face."

Brett Wallace had done both and moved on. His third life was the one which had to count. He relearned and perfected all the ninja ways; *Kuji-kiri*, the art of distraction; *Chikairi-no-jutsu*, the art of infiltration; *Shuriken-jutsu*, the art of throwing; *Yogen-jutsu*, the art of chemical warfare; *Yubijutsu*, the art of death by fingers. And even *saiminjutsu*, the art of suggestion and imagination.

But mostly he learned about himself. He learned just how brilliant was the human mind and how capable was the human body. He learned the truth behind the quote of Shakespeare: "What a piece of work is man." For every moment he spent honing his martial skills, he spent five honing his mental ones. Not only did he learn techniques of incredible devastation, but ones of amazing dexterity, subtlety, and gentleness. By the end of his year there he could not only turn stones into powder with his fist but he could perform the *sado*—the tea ceremony—with a grace that was literally stunning.

"Now you are truly a ninja," Torii declared happily, all the more pleased that they had saved a loved one who seemed intent on some sort of *seppuku*—or hari-kiri as it was more commonly known. If the truth be known hari-kiri was something commoners did. The rite of *seppuku* was reserved for the warrior class. "Remember," Master Torii continued. "You are now no one and everyone. Your true art is how you blend and become invisible whether you are in a crowd or an open field. You exist to right wrongs and you will continue to do so as long as you remember that you are the most important person in your life. You cannot right wrongs if exposed. And an exposed ninja is not a ninja at all. He is a dead man."

"I will never forget," Brett promised his teacher.

"Go," said Master Torii. With that, the little man who was probably the most deadly creation on the face of the earth turned his back and walked deeper into the Chiba garden until Brett could no longer see him. He would never see him again.

"Come," said Yamaguchi. "I will take you to the airport."

They rode in calm silence until they nearly reached the Tokyo airport almost two hours later. Then Yamaguchi pulled off the main road and stopped outside a little shop at the end of a long, thin alleyway. He motioned that Brett should follow him. The pair walked inside the dank store to see a wizened old man seated behind a counter reading a comic book. He looked up when the two ninja entered, locked gazes with Yamaguchi, smiled a toothless smile, then hopped through a curtain in the back wall. The master followed him and Brett did likewise.

Beyond the curtain was a fenced-in yard that even had a corrugated steel roof over it. There were some doors in the back fence and in front of those doors—incredibly—was a dead cow. A few yards in front of the cow was a table with two long, wrapped packages.

The old, toothless man picked up the longer of the two packages and stripped off the newspaper covering it. Beneath that was green cloth carefully tied at the top. The man gingerly picked at the knot until it came apart. The cloth fell away from a beautiful samurai sword—a *katana*.

It was done almost all in sumptuous black—a black that seemed to glisten with a life all its own. But once the old man pulled the sword from its scabbard, the lustrous black was diminished by the vivid sheen of the incredibly sharp blade.

"An authentic samurai sword is made by joining hard

and soft metal to an amazingly thin edge," explained Yamaguchi, "then folded at least thirty times to give it strength. A good katana is at least fifty folds."

The old man took the sword in both hands and approached the middle of the dead cow.

"Before a master swordsmith delivers his blade," Yamaguchi continued, "he must give it a final test. Just a hundred years ago or so, the blade's failure here might mean the blade-maker's death."

Brett watched as the old man reared back, then sliced the cow in two right down the center. The animal might have been warm butter and the blade a sledgehammer for all the resistance it was given. The old man cackled, hopped from one foot to the other, then turned to bring the sword back to the table. After he carefully cleaned it and lovingly placed it back within its scabbard and cloth cover, he presented it to Yamaguchi with his head bowed.

"No," the master instructed in Japanese. "Present them to their rightful owner."

The old man looked up and turned to Brett, who was staring at Yamaguchi. The old man gathered up the shorter sword, and fell on his knees before the American. He held the two blades up in supplication.

"By rights they must be yours," Yamaguchi told him. "Besides your being, they are your only connection to us and your true home."

Brett was overwhelmed and he finally understood completely. The name Brett Wallace now meant nothing. He was ninja, part of a family that had lived at the heart of the Orient for hundreds of years. His past families were dead. But he would always belong to the ninja—now and through eternity. He took the swords without reserve or embarrassment. They felt like two arms he had always been missing.

"Thank you, Teacher," he said.

"No *teacher* nor *master* now," Yamaguchi said. "You are one of us."

Traveling alone back to the United States, Brett reflected on all of the things he had learned. He remembered the all-encompassing calm that blanketed him whenever he was perfectly ready. He remembered back to when his blood had rushed and he had tensed whenever he entered battle. He now existed within a realm of peace and an assurance of complete capability. He was all that he could be. If he were killed now, it would not be because he made himself less a man.

He had achieved a oneness with himself and he would create a new life-style to support that oneness and make it grow.

He did not need to turn down the various drinks, snacks, and bad food the airline stewardesses were constantly foisting on the passengers. No matter how many times one came by, she never seemed to notice Brett. Everyone around him would get their dry-roasted nuts in the foil pouch and their little plastic glasses of liquid, but somehow the flight attendants never saw him. He couldn't help but smile at the crew's look of confusion when they said a hesitant good-bye to him at the door once the plane landed in San Francisco. Up until then, they apparently didn't even know he was on the flight.

Brett remembered what Torii had said. "A ninja is not seen. He lets himself be seen."

Rhea was waiting for him in the passenger's lounge. She was five-five—tall for an Oriental woman—and twenty-seven years old. But like many of her compatriots, she seemed eternally young. She would probably look about the same in twenty-seven more years. And she looked beautiful. Almond eyes, small nose, full lips, and a wide-breasted, Occidentally shaped body. Her hair was as black and rich as his samurai swords.

They approached each other calmly but once they had met and kissed, their passion was deep and unmistakable. They had made a commitment to each other far greater than marriage. They were now inseparable parts of each other's lives.

She looked up at him. Unknown to anyone and almost impossible for anyone else to achieve, each eye locked onto its counterpart. There was no focusing of both eyes on one eye of the other's. Brett's right eye looked directly into Rhea's left and his left eye directly into her right.

"I've missed you, my love," she told him. He kissed her again. "Nice to have you back," she said with a smile when they finally drew apart.

"Nice to be back," he said.

On the way to the restaurant, Brett thought about how his life would change. Outwardly it would seem as if the Brett Wallace so many saw out on the town would disappear. But inwardly, not much else would be different. He wouldn't drink, but he would still cook, only now it too was an art which he would practice for others. He would still create wildly exotic dishes, but he wouldn't taste them. He would know if they were perfect simply by smell.

As soon as he settled in the Rhea Dawn office he assigned Rhea power of attorney, making her the official executor of Brett's father's estate. She owned the restaurant and had the power to turn the Dawn Dojo over to Jeff Archer, which she did. As soon as that was accomplished, she got some designers working on the two establishments as per Brett's instructions. The immediate money she needed to pay the builders came from the sale of Brett's Sausalito house.

Within a few months a special loft was built over the restaurant and a special basement was finished under the dojo. Brett's new schedule started immediately after that. Every morning somewhere between four and six-thirty he would meet Jeff at the martial arts studio and go downstairs for an intense round of mutual instruction. The cellar was now a broad room which looked like a giant coffin. It was sixty feet long and twenty feet high. Along every wall were cases of martial arts implements as well as targets and special constructions. There, Brett showed Jeff the new way while maintaining his own skills.

Jeff Archer was an apt, honest, and eager pupil. He was twenty-five years old and five feet, nine inches worth of wiry, lithely muscled flesh. His face was triangular and handsome in a boyish sort of way. His hair was brown and wavy but he kept it cut pretty short. His eyes were also brown and somehow gave the impression that they had seen more than they should. Jeff had a right to this impression—his grandmother had been burned alive by a gang of hoods—a gang Jeff had failed to defeat, but one which Brett had eliminated shortly after they met. It was that meeting which led to the co-owned dojo—the one that Archer now owned completely.

The young man was serious about his responsibility and grew both as a martial artist and a teacher. With Brett's directions, he stressed the Zen, Tao, and other philosophy of the martial arts more than the ability to break bricks with one's head. Those students who were out for a thrill or to acquire a destructive ability were soon weeded out by that approach. Archer's courses took homework, and not just the kind where a student smacks his fist against a wall until his knuckles bleed. The Dawn Dojo demanded that serious students know Oriental art, poetry, literature, medicine, and science before they got their black belts.

Within weeks of the new direction, the two had worked out a personal regimen. Once he had arrived, Brett would kick the wall and punch a box of stones until Jeff showed up with a bowl of fruit and walnuts. Once every few weeks Archer could be seen dumping out a box of dust into the garbage. Anyone seeing him wouldn't know that the dust was once rocks Brett had been pounding with his bare hands. Anyone seeing Archer move the special steel, plexiglass, and wood panels into the dojo wouldn't know that they were to protect the rapidly crumbling wall Brett had been kicking, either.

After those limbering up exercises, the two would stand across the way from each other. Jeff would throw the hard shelled nuts which Brett would catch between his thumb and forefinger. Then he would crush them. Next Brett would unwrap his katana and Jeff would grab an armful of different fruits. One after another he'd throw them to Brett, who would peel them with his blade before they hit the ground. Grapefruit was fairly easy. Oranges were no sweat. It was when he got down to the apples and grapes that things got intense. Brett didn't try to peel those completely—an effort he succeeded with on the citrus fruit—he just tried to cut away some of the skin without touching the meat.

After a while he succeeded at that too. Then Jeff would throw the fruit faster and faster. Within a few months, Brett was slicing this way and that—almost faster than the eye could follow—perfectly exposing piece after piece of uncut fruit under the sliced skin. After that came the system. Jeff would roll out six bamboo poles, each laid flat out on a table, in front of a large chunk of wood. Brett would move to the opposite end of the room, all sixty feet away and take out a short bow and arrows—the *kyusen*—in preparation. Then he would place six *shuriken* and six long cords on various areas of his body.

On Jeff's word, he would rapidly fire the six arrows so they went right through each successive bamboo tube without touching the sides and sink into the wooden slat, then even as Jeff was pulling the table of tubes out of the way, Brett would hurl all six *shuriken* so that they clove each successive arrow in twain, and then he would hurl each cord to wrap around each *shuriken*. With a tug, each five-pointed star would pop out of the wall.

By that time Jeff would be needed upstairs to open the studio. After the young man had left, Brett would approach a special floor section which was done in the slickest tile available. He would keep this section so freshly waxed that most people couldn't walk across it without slipping. Then he covered the floor section with the cheapest toilet paper he could buy—the kind he thought would tear if you looked at it wrong. Then he would spray the whole thing with water vapor so the tissue was practically transparent.

Finally he would run back and forth across the section without wrinkling or tearing the toilet paper. Then he would run backwards across it. Then sideways. All without ruffling the sodden tissue in the least. When finished Brett left by a special exit so no one coming in for classes would pass him. Then he would walk back to the restaurant, rain or shine, carefully noting how the rest of civilization was getting on. He would study the walk and associated movement of almost everyone he saw: the old man bent with arthritis; the old woman weighed down with packages; the young girls flying kites in the park; the young men throwing Frisbees; the businessmen on their way to work; the children toddling next to their patient or long-suffering mothers. Nothing escaped his study, not even the animals; dogs, cats, and birds. He examined all their actions, reactions, and movements to develop his repertoire of stealth.

All of those he studied hardly noticed him. There was nothing spectacular about him. He was a plain, well-built, medium-height man with medium-length sandy hair and steel gray eyes. He wore simple, unassuming clothes and comfortable shoes. He had no jewelry, not even a watch. He knew what time it was.

If he let five people see him all at once, there would probably be five descriptions of him once he disappeared. He wasn't ugly, but he wasn't striking. He wasn't plain, but he wasn't spectacular either. He could be anybody and he certainly intended to be.

The restaurant had a special entrance for him as well. He could come in through the kitchen door in the back or the side door. He would occasionally enter with the rest of the patrons, but no one took any undue notice of him. He made sure of it. The Brett Wallace many diners would be sure that they had recognized from somewhere had now drifted into the shadows—even in the brightest daylight. He would even be able to meet Lynn McDonald again and honestly convince her that he was not who she thought he was.

This day Brett came in the front door since it wasn't eleven-thirty yet and the restaurant wasn't open for business. He was wearing jeans, a blue t-shirt, and a tan corduroy jacket. He had boat sneakers on his feet. The Rhea Dawn was a beautiful place. Decorated mostly in teak and beautiful calligraphy, it seemed airy and light at all times. Rhea had the help wear traditional Japanese outfits and every employee was old world Oriental. Within that criteria it was an equal opportunity employer. Rhea would take on Japanese, Chinese, Korean, and all the other yellow-skinned races.

Brett went through the bustling kitchen which was already preparing for the lunch crowd. He waved at Hama, their affable cook. Hama smiled as he kept most of his attention on the various woks and pots. Brett trotted up to his special dining antechamber to find Rhea in a kimono sipping tea and poring over the morning newspapers.

"Anything interesting?" Brett asked, sitting next to her across the butcher's block table.

"The same old thing, I'm afraid," she said from behind the paper. "Not much we can do about the shrinking dollar."

"How's the yen?" he asked, rising and going over to a section of the wall which was attached to the kitchen below by a modern dumbwaiter system.

"Solid as Sony," she replied, putting the paper down flat atop the pile of other news sources. She leaned back and sipped her tea with both hands while scanning the *New York Times* op-ed page. It was tilted up to her eyes by stacked copies of the *Los Angeles Times,* the *Dallas Examiner,* the *Washington Star, Time, Newsweek, U.S. News and World Report, Forbes, Fortune,* the *London Times, Paris Match,* the *Pravda Report,* and the week's issues of the *Congressional Record.*

Brett slipped open a section of the wall and pulled out a small tray Hama had sent up as soon as he saw Wallace enter. On it was a variety of fish, some various broths, and a bowl of non-fat milk. He took it and walked past the table, casually closing Rhea's newspaper as he went. "Come on, then," he told her and started up a stairway that was just a few feet from the steps he had climbed to get into the antechamber.

Rhea left the *New York Times* with the rest of the reading material and went up the stairs after Brett. The two emerged into a large loft which stretched the entire length of the building. Every inch of the twelve-foot-high walls was covered with books. The floor was solid oak occasionally interrupted by a supporting beam which stretched to the ceiling. On this wooden floor—carefully covered with fireproof plastic which seemed part of the wood itself—were different sections of living space. To the immediate right was a large, carefully stocked kitchen. To the left a just as carefully decked-out eating area. Both were designed to make a meal a ceremony—an event. For Brett, it had to be that way. He only allowed himself one meal a day.

Enclosed next to the kitchen was the bath, a magnificent structure which housed a shower, a steam room, a bathtub, and a redwood tub. The toilet and sink were closed off next to that. Finally there was a sleeping and meditation corner. It had a mat, a platform bed, and a water bed. Brett could sleep anywhere, on any surface, but when he chose to sleep, he preferred a variety at hand. To the left of all that was the biggest section of the space. The entertainment and computer center.

Brett shared more than his martial arts with the Orient. His secret, guilty passion was a love of gadgets. Amid the towering array of devices in this section, there was not one machine with the words Zenith or General Electric on it. There was Panasonic, Hitachi, Sony, Toshiba, and mostly NEC—Nippon Electric. But in his case, this passion served a purpose. As he so painfully learned, a ninja was more than just a master of death. He was a master of life—a man who knew more about the world around him than any of his contemporaries. That's what gave him the edge. That's what truly made him capable of killing any opponent he faced. Instinctively he knew what that person would do before or as they were doing it.

And that instinct was fueled by knowledge—The knowledge of everything. Not only had Brett's physical capabilities grown, but so had his mental abilities. He could digest, understand, and use more information in a day than anyone else could do in a week of concerted effort. The Nippon Electric computer he had designed for himself supplemented his need for knowledge greatly. It took weeks for Brett to ingest what he needed to know about computer language so he could hook up his incredible system to some of the most private information sources available, but he had done it. The large color screen and paper read-out devices pumped a surprising amount of secret as well as seemingly useless information into Brett's loft.

Not only did the computer collect the information, but upon Brett's instruction, it organized and analyzed it. He could set up an extraordinary amount of cross-references. The man sat down in his chair opposite the machine, bit into a fresh shrimp and started the material going.

"The statistics are remaining consistent for this time of year," Rhea told him while examining the typed read-out. "With the increase in temperature there is a proportionate increase in violent crime. Murder, as always, is up."

"There's little I can do for the dead," Brett said solemnly as the green-tinged information rattled across and rolled up his television screen. He popped some unprocessed tuna into his mouth. "Rape?" he asked.

"Down," Rhea reported, slightly surprised.

"Is that just today or does it hold to some kind of pattern?" Brett inquired without turning from the TV.

"It fluctuates," Rhea told him, "but there seems to be a definite trend downward on the East Coast."

As always, Brett pounced upon any inconsistency and traced it down to its possible source. With his right hand he reached across the keyboard which was permanently installed in the table next to his chair and tapped out orders that the NEC computer should concentrate on East Coast reports. Local newspapers, doctors' private files, public records, and police reports, among many others, were all collected and evaluated by Brett's precise computer program. The machine started running down a list of possible connections.

"More Government assistance to the New York City welfare system seems to have quieted things down a bit," Rhea mused. Brett did not answer. Something was gnawing at the back of his brain. Rape itself did not have to be down, it was only the instances of reported rapes that saw any change. And a rape wouldn't be reported if the victim were scared, shamed, or in no shape to report anything to anybody.

"Disappearances," Brett said aloud while tapping the information out on the keys. "I want a list of those missing on the entire East Coast since the beginning of the month and the most immediate vital statistics that come to mind."

Rhea looked up from the read-out. "This will be one of your marathons, won't it?"

"I'll see you tonight, my love," Brett replied with little whimsy. "Have a good day."

Rhea moved away from the print-out machine and silently went behind Brett's back to the various wardrobe enclosures between the dining area and the entertainment center. She opened the enclosure's door while letting her kimono fall to the floor. She was naked beneath it, but Brett did not turn around to take in her sleek, creamy beauty. She pulled on a peach-colored teddi and slipped on some simple heels. Over those she shrugged into a simple floral print wrap dress. Ready to face the work day, she looked sadly toward the television and the back of Brett's head.

Marching down the screen was a seemingly endless list of missing persons. Under each name were sections for age, race, occupation, address, and "comments." These comments were usually notes collected by the police from friends, neighbors, and relatives in terms of possible clues. Before Rhea left to manage the lunch crowd downstairs, she saw comments that ranged from the sad to the pitiful to the ludicrous. It was a march of pain and waste, put into words and completely ingested by the ninja master.

Rhea was beautiful even when she perspired and after ten hours of marching from the kitchen to the dining rooms and back again, there was a thin sheen of sweat that made her skin glow just under her neck and right above her cleavage. She was sweating over a steaming vat of won ton soup in the restaurant kitchen. When she looked up she saw Brett standing on the other side of the stove through the mist.

As soon as the cloud cleared and she saw the expression on his face, she knew that he had something new. "What is it, Brett?"

"We have a meeting tomorrow morning," he told her. "I've already called Jeff. Tell Hama I'll need detailed reports on arms traffic from the Virginia-Pennsylvania line to Richmond. I'll also need detailed road maps of the same area. I'll be up cross checking police reports. Good night."

Another burst of heat rose up from the won ton blocking Rhea's view for a second. When she brushed the steam away, Brett was already gone. She sighed. She had a feeling he would be leaving her again for another protracted length of time.

The next morning found Hama, Rhea, and Jeff seated around Brett's dining table while Brett himself stood in front of the computer-connected TV screen with a small remote control box in his hand. In front of Jeff was a glass of orange juice and a stack of manila envelope files, in front of Rhea was a cup of herb tea and a bunch of maps, and in front of Hama was a bottle of Scotch and some note pads. Hama was a chubby little man with a large, wide forehead who was always dressed in white karate pants and a sleeveless white T-shirt. The only hint of his inner strength was his eyes and his tight biceps which rumbled out just below his hard shoulders.

Seemingly complacent and gentle, Hama was not only a fine cook, but an expert with every sort of non-Oriental weapon. He kept Brett completely up to date on every new killing machine manufactured by human ingenuity. So, when the ninja had to face one he knew exactly how many pounds of thrust it took to pull the trigger, exactly what kind of ammunition might be heading toward him and at what speed, and exactly what kind of weaknesses the killing machine had.

"Dierdre Peterson," said Brett, electronically calling up a variety of photos on the TV screen. The trio at the table saw a handsome girl with a thin face and flaxen hair. "A beginning real estate agent anxious to make her first sale. Variously described as 'flighty,' 'flirtatious,' and 'over-eager.' Went out on a job from an office in Baltimore and never came back."

Brett clicked the remote control again to bring up a variety of photos of an attractive brunette. One was a high-school graduation picture, one was a résumé photo, and a third was a blurry press picture of her at a New York party. "Tanya Bauer," Brett explained, "an actress who took a job with a film company as technical assistant to pay the bills. Went to scout locations for a independent feature called 'Blood Village' and never came back."

" 'Blood Village?' " Jeff echoed incredulously.

"Yeah," Brett said with a vague air of disgust. "You know. One of those 'knife-kill' movies with a bunch of crazy yahoo's slaughtering all the young girls they can find."

"And we wonder why things are getting so dangerous in this country," Rhea mused.

"It's all entertainment," Hama quietly interjected, his hands behind his head and his eyes staring at the ceiling. "Boys take their dates to them so they can squeal and cuddle."

"And the minorities go to blow off steam and yell at the screen," Jeff added.

"Back to the real world, boys and girls," Brett admonished, calling up a final set of pictures. These portrayed college yearbook photos of dances, mixers, social activities, plays, and sporting events. In every shot was at least two of four teens; two attractive girls and two attractive boys. "Tom Murphy, Larry Langer, Terri Cunningham, and Carol Kirkland," Brett detailed. "Four students who told their classmates that they were going to do a little camping 'up north' from their Richmond campus. Left on a Friday, never seen again."

"A girl from Maryland, one from Manhattan, and some kids from college," Jeff summed up. "What do they have in common?"

"A town called Tylerville," Brett answered, coming back to the table.

"Why Tylerville?" Rhea wanted to know.

"Originally called Cannon Crossing," Brett told her, dropping the remote control on the table's wood surface and putting both palms down flat. "A very small town nestled at the base of a small mountain. Used as a depot for Revolutionary War armaments. That's where it got its original name. Since then its been underpopulated, mostly by retirees who couldn't afford to live anyplace else. Then, in 1966 the entire town was bought lock, stock, and barrel by a corporation owned by Nathan Garrard Tyler."

Hama whistled up at the ceiling. "Tylerville," Jeff repeated. "Of course."

"Of course," Brett agreed. "And all of a sudden a whole new population seems to spring up. Mostly cops are listed on the town's payroll, but there's also a rather interesting list of educators, educational assistants, and student counselors listed as Tyler employees."

"What for?" Rhea wanted to know. "Tyler is a big business mystery man. All the magazines know about him is that he seemed to appear full blown in the middle sixties with a stupendous bankroll support to start a scientific research and counseling service. Then, as soon as his son, Steven, got old enough, he served as the company's spokesman. It doesn't seem logical that Tyler would start spreading the word of his success through EST-like encounter groups or anything like that."

"He isn't," Brett informed her. "He's sinking millions of dollars into a humanitarian effort. After buying the town, he moved his central corporation offices there and started construction on a school. A free school for the education of orphans. Not only is this place a good public relations move but an excellent tax shelter. So he opens his doors for orphans to come from all over America for free, and all of a sudden people start to disappear."

"But these people could've disappeared anywhere in Northern Virginia," Jeff complained. "Why pick Tylerville?"

Brett picked up the remote control with one hand and held up the forefinger of his other hand. As dozens of names started appearing across the TV screen, he spoke. "First, because almost none of these 'educational assistants' and counselors seem to have any background in the teaching business. Mostly they are names of his previous employees in completely different departments. Second, Tylerville's police department. It seems to outnumber the residents. Hama?"

The Oriental cook came down from his examination of the ceiling, took his hands from behind his head and started riffling through the books in front of him absentmindedly. "Naturally there's no legal move of heavy arms into the town," he reported, "but my sources assure me that the black market trade in guns and ammunition is booming in Tylerville. The actual expenditure is not that great, but compared to the amount of firepower that was used in the town before Tyler bought it, it seems warfare is positively booming around the mountain."

"What kind of stuff are we talking about?" Jeff inquired.

"Oh, before 1966 there was one or two shotguns about," Hama told him. "Just some simple hunting weapons used by the locals. But since Tyler moved in there's been a steadily increasing amount of sales for .45 automatics, .357 and .44 Magnums, Browning 9mm's, and even such nasty automatic machine guns as the MAC 10 and 11's and the Israeli Uzi."

"Intimidation guns," Jeff commented.

"You bet," Hama answered. You could look down the barrel of any one of those and see your life go by in Cinerama."

"But this town is supposed to be the Tyler corporate headquarters now," Rhea piped in, playing the devil's advocate. "It would make sense that he guard himself carefully."

"Perhaps," Brett agreed, "but from all the material I was able to get from the NEC it seems that the 'corporate headquarters' title is just a cover for the Tyler family's home base. Outside of Tyler and his son, the only other corporate employees stationed there are the cops and 'educational assistants.' "

"I'm still not convinced completely," Rhea maintained. She had joined in three summit meetings like this one since Brett had destroyed the street gang that had killed Archer's grandmother and all had ended up being false alarms. Upon investigation, the ninja master had discovered no more corruption and wrongdoing than usual. "What makes you so sure that these disappearances can be tied in with Tylerville?"

"The arrest reports," Brett replied with a small degree of triumph. With a click, he had the computer start pumping the material out across the television screen. "Since the beginning of the year every town in Northern Virginia— even the towns comparatively sized to Tylerville—show the arrest or questioning of a young person; specifically a girl between the ages of sixteen and thirty. In Tylerville, nothing. Absolutely nothing."

"An armed town is a polite town?" Hama paraphrased an old saying as way of explanation.

"I cross-checked and double-checked the Tylerville police reports since the town's inception in 1966," Brett told them. "The latest report is exactly the same as the report delivered in the same week of 1972. Last month's arrest reports were exactly the same as those exactly ten years prior. These guys are sending the same reports that they sent a decade ago with new names and dates on them!"

Brett's three associates looked around the table at each other. No one had to go into detail as to what they were thinking. Something was wrong in Tylerville. Something that Brett Wallace was intent on finding out.

"I'll need a soda truck," he told Rhea. "One thing these little towns have plenty of is bars. A man offering to sell them cola at fifty percent under the cost of Coke or Pepsi won't be suspected right away."

"How soon?" asked Rhea.

"Delivery by the end of the week," Brett replied, standing in front of the TV, which was still displaying cross-referenced police reports. "I'll need time to prepare."

For the next few days, Brett had Jeff intensify his exercises. When he wasn't training, Brett was working at the tiny lab in the dojo cellar and poring over every scrap of information he could get concerning the physical layout of Tylerville and several of the towns surrounding it. On Friday the old truck was delivered in New York. That night Brett took a cross-country flight. The next morning he set off. Within two days he was in Tylerville. His first stop after some careful sightseeing was Stan's Tavern.

Chapter Three

They came for her at night as usual. At first she kept from facing her situation by screaming hysterically whenever anyone came near. And, at first, her captors had just laughed and laughed at her hysteria, watching her naked body buck on the bed. But then, when they wanted to talk with her, two men would grab her head and blonde hair while a third taped her mouth shut. Then he would do whatever he wanted with her.

This night was different, however. The men still moved silently into her cell and slapped the sticky material across her mouth before she woke up and he still sat on the edge of the bed, caressing her as he spoke, but tonight he told her his name.

"Call me Steven," he suggested as she desperately tried to escape the padded leather shackles that held her spread-eagled across the mattress. "No, no, you shouldn't fight," he admonished. "You should consider yourself very lucky. You're not like the others. All of them are so ugly. Not like you. You're perfect." He stroked her hair and cupped her chin as the other men stood behind the bed, their eyes sparkling.

"All the orphans didn't do anything for me one way or the other," he continued as she struggled in the dim light. "They were for Daddy, anyway. Everything is always for Daddy. So I did a little hunting on my own . . . with my friends." He looked back to his associates and smiled. They nodded like the little toy dogs that shake their heads in the back windows of cars.

"The first one was a little too old. She was nice, but crazy. I gave her to Daddy. The second was really nice but not very tough. She broke almost right away. You're great, though. It was worth getting rid of your friends to get to you."

Terri Cunningham thought she might go mad. She tore crazily at her bonds and tried to scream herself hoarse. She only succeeded in tearing the skin around her mouth, wrists, and ankles. Steven turned around and snapped his fingers. One of his associates handed him a small case. Steven studiously opened it and took out one of those modern, needleless syringes—the kind that pumps the medicine into the arm.

"Hold her," Steven instructed. The three men pressed down on her legs, stomach and arms. Steven placed the barrel and pulled the trigger. Terri felt a hunk of something sweep into her veins from her upper right arm. Whatever it was seemed to cover her body like a wave, making all her limbs feel full of gravel. In seconds she felt as if she were floating. The easy, soothing sensation terrified her all the more, but the horror went no further than her brain. Her body was no longer responding.

Her vision clouded and she saw her boyfriend and the other college couple back in the woods, across from the camp fire they had built. She saw Carol's laughing face framed by her brown, curly hair. She saw Tom and Larry horsing around by the tents. Then, in slow motion almost, she saw the other men with their shotguns coming toward her. They took forever to get close but even so Terri could not get away. She sat and watched as the boys were blown apart like red water balloons and Carol was set upon by hundreds of hands. Carol's mouth opened in silent surprise until it seemed to take up her whole face. There was just a gigantic mouth hole framed by huge brown eyes where her face used to be. And there were only hundreds of fingers wiggling where her body once was. They looked like large blood worms with joints burrowing into her body.

Terri Cunningham cried as Steven Tyler pulled the tape off of her mouth. She felt the pain and opened her eyes to groggily study his visage. It was a sharply etched face with high cheekbones, a thin nose, thin lips, black hair, and blue eyes. But on top of this sharp face were incongruous hunks of fatty flesh—as if the young man was already going to seed. It was a mean face which seemed to promise a limitless capability for evil. Terri opened her mouth to scream but the drug let no sound come out.

"Don't be like that," Steven warned. "You should be nice to me. I have the complete power of life and death over you. And there's not a damn thing anybody can do about that."

And then he shoved his tongue down her throat.

Brett Wallace dumped the bodies of the three rapists into the chairs they had been sitting in at Stan's tavern. Then he pulled some more bullets out of Andy's gun belt, carefully loaded the .357 Magnum revolver and blew all three men away. He shot them in different places so the aim would not look so precise. The whole scene, however, looked as if Olivia had gotten her hands on the sawed-off shotgun first, killed Stan and Andy, then got the deputy's revolver and murdered the three patrons.

Brett left the bar, passing the van he had used to drive the men back to the tavern. Then he ran back to the soda truck which he had hidden among the trees. Naturally, had the girl been awake, she wouldn't have seen or heard his approach. But having relaxed her with a few acupuncture grips, Olivia was sleeping fitfully, if not peacefully, in the curtained-off section between the truck's cab and the payload area. Her jeans had been in one piece so she had put those on, while they were able to create a makeshift halter top out of her ripped shirt.

Brett soundlessly slipped into the driver's seat, still wearing his dark blue ninja hood over his facial features. He quickly started the engine and brought the truck back out onto the road, heading north out of town—the way he had come. He mentally replayed the information Olivia had given him. Although he had rescued her, another beautiful black woman, Rosalind Cole, was still captive somewhere in town. And as far as Olivia knew, she was being held in jail or at the sheriff's house.

The theory Brett had been working on all along was taking firmer shape in his mind. The sheriff had gone a little power mad with the money Tyler was paying him. He set up the sort of system that small town lawmen were known for. By bribing the judges and the wardens he could stop almost anyone he took a fancy to on a trumped-up charge and see to it that they are incarcerated in a backwoods prison with no hope of release and no recourse but to serve the sheriff's wishes if they wanted to survive. Brett wanted to get this young model to safety and then move in on the jail to free the fashion editor and exact vengeance on their attackers.

He rounded the curve to the final stretch of road out of town. To his surprise there were three patrol cars blocking the way with six heavily armed cops waving flashlights at him to pull over.

Now he knew how Mel felt when he saw the soda truck. Only Brett's face and body gave no hint of his surprise. His mind raced across various explanations even as his body moved.

They couldn't have found the bodies at Stan's tavern this fast unless someone had heard the shots and had a CB radio to report the discovery right away. But Brett knew that there were no houses nearby since he had made a thorough study and reconnaissance of the area before he moved in. He also knew that there were no vehicles on the road within hearing range save his own. And unless someone was hunting grouse in the woods at two o'clock in the morning, the five deaths were still undiscovered.

There was another reason for the roadblock. Brett couldn't waste time figuring out what it was. First and foremost he had to make sure no one saw him and the sheriff didn't get his paws on Olivia.

Brett spun the wide, heavy wheel of the truck with one hand as if he were spinning a bottle while pulling up on the hand brake with the other. The truck locked wheels, screeched sideways, spun its tail in the direction it had been moving in, bounced up on two wheels, then finally landed pointed in the opposite direction. Brett released the brake, and slammed down on the accelerator. The back wheels spun madly, bit into the asphalt and leaped forward —away from the police cars.

Brett glanced into the rear view mirror. Sure enough, the half dozen cops dove for their vehicles. That was all he saw before he rounded the corner and sped back into town.

Damn, he thought. If only I had more time to prepare! The sudden arrival of the girl was unexpected. Brett had originally planned to worm his way into the confidence of various townspeople and observe the whole process of whatever was going down. But bad timing and coincidence had forced him into action earlier than anticipated. It wasn't so much that he minded fighting so early, it was just that coming on this strong this fast might endanger the lives of the missing . . . if they weren't already dead.

Brett heard the sirens of the cop cars chasing him. Instantaneously his sharp hearing noted that only two of the three cars were hot in pursuit. They had left a final car to remain at the Tylerville border. Brett was now positive. The blockade wasn't meant for him alone. It was meant for anyone who tried to leave the town at night. Suddenly his theory of legal corruption seemed incomplete. A greater piece of the picture was missing.

That piece seemed all the more important when he heard the sounds of gunfire behind him. He looked in the rearview mirror again. The police cars were streaking up behind him while trying to blow out his rear tires. He wondered what kind of maniacs wore badges in this town. Anywhere else the police had to account for every spent shell in triplicate. Here they were dotting the roadway with lead.

Another thing struck him. They could have easily overtaken the truck and almost anyone who spent a rudimentary amount of time on a firing range could have hit the big truck wheels, but these guys seemed to be covering their eyes and pulling triggers anyway they wanted. Even after he counted eight reports, the truck didn't seem damaged in any way.

The cops seemed to be needlessly and dangerously toying with a culprit they knew nothing about. If what Olivia had told him was true then the pursuing cops didn't know about her and they were blasting away for the hell of it. Any other man would have been stunned at this realization. Brett merely readjusted his thinking. He wasn't dealing with a dragnet to catch a single terrified girl. He was dealing with a curfew. To break it was to risk death.

With all his abilities, Brett couldn't make the truck go faster. Staying on the road meant certain capture or certain slaughter. He would have to weave and dodge until he could be sure that the chasing cops weren't calling the rest of the Tylerville cavalry on top of him. He didn't doubt that he might be able to defeat them all, but his massacre would only serve to seal the fate of the innocents involved. He couldn't play his full hand now.

Brett spun the wheel again with the miraculous ease that would have impressed anyone. But instead of spinning the vehicle all the way around as before, he set it on a course toward the woods to the left of the road. The truck teetered on two wheels again, then made a vicious arc for the trees. The cop cars were taken by surprise, overshooting Brett's turn-off point by several hundred feet. They screeched to a tire-burning halt, took a second to understand what had happened, then burned rubber toward the forest after the soda truck.

Brett concentrated all his skill on barreling the truck

66

through what little clear space there was. The way, which had been smooth up until then, became a rolling sea of rocks, felled branches, and steep inclines. The cab tossed and bucked like a tug boat in the middle of a monsoon. Despite the acupuncture treatment, the trip couldn't help but awaken the girl. Brett heard her little cries of fear and surprise.

"Stay back," he told her, remaining glued to his seat. "Hold on and keep down."

The truck smashed over a fallen tree. The front tires bounced up and over, bringing the cab crashing down. For the first time Brett's rear left the seat but his head did not touch the ceiling—such was his muscular control. The rear wheels ground against the tree trunk a few seconds before they caught and hurled the vehicle on its way. It then jumped over the lip of a hill, flew down ten feet then crashed back to the dirt, sending up gouts of brown dust clouds in its wake.

The two cop cars tore into the hole the truck had made in the brush. They too slammed into the tree trunk, but they did not have the height of the bigger rig. One car's tires smashed into the wood bar, spun madly—slicing off yards of bark—then peeled off to the right. The other car hit the fallen tree head on, smashing all its headlights before it jumped up and over the obstruction.

Both cars made it past, only to face the treacherous dirt hill. The car coursing to the right lost its grip and slid down the embankment sideways, completely out of control. The other car smashed down on the hill's lip, bounced, and did a swan dive across half the declining distance. It landed nose first, pushing the ruined headlights into the engine. The motor cracked, sputtered and died.

The slipping car came to a rest at the bottom of the hill, damaged, but not dead. The driver stuck his head out the window and yelled to the officers in the useless auto. "Come on! We'll all go after 'im!"

"Forget it!" came the return yell. "We'll radio ahead. Find out what the fuck is goin' on!"

The first yeller didn't argue the point further. Tearing

up the ground with his spinning tires, the remaining active vehicle continued pursuit.

Brett ground the truck up the incline on the other side of the hill. He felt the big tires dig into the boulders that covered the way as it slowly managed the climb. All he wanted to do was get away from the police cars, then he could stash the truck and make an escape by foot. It would be easier that way. The truck finally made it to the top of the new obstruction with an almost painful last push. Brett was about to send the rig forward at top speed when he saw that they had run out of road. All that was in front of them was a drop of some fifty feet. In a vehicle this heavy, the fall would be fatal.

The ninja spun the wheel again, listening carefully for the sound of the police cars' approach. He only heard one coming up from the right. He threw subtlety out the window. It would be stretching his scenario a bit, but he had little choice. He pulled his steering wheel to the right and tapped the accelerator. Cautiously, the truck began to inch in that direction along the very lip of the cliff. Any sudden speed might crumble what little leverage they had and send the vehicle in a nose dive to major damage.

The sound of the chasing car came closer. Brett continued to twist the wheel and touch the pedal. The truck creaked and complained but it continued to move right without disaster. Finally Brett had it facing directly to the right—safe on the narrow space between the hill and the cliff. Brett cut the headlights off just as the cop car screeched up onto the same space, facing in his direction.

Without waiting, Brett jammed the accelerator to the floor. He didn't give the cops a chance to stop or swerve. The front of the soda truck rammed into the cop car right behind its left headlight. The truck kept barreling forward, pushing the auto along the ledge in front of it. Brett saw the driver tumble into the back seat. He saw the passenger cop whack his head against the dashboard and fall back.

He looked beyond the crumbling police car he was pushing. Just twenty yards ahead, the ledge curved to the left, leaving another cliff face. Brett only had to hurl the car that far and the sharp drop would do all his work for him. He looked back to the rending car in time to see rationality return to the second cop's eyes. He saw the cop level his pump shotgun at the truck through his own windshield.

Brett only had time to say, "Down!" Then he ducked himself before both glass partitions were blasted. The hole in the cop car windshield was about a foot wide. The spreading shotgun pellets took out one half of the truck's glass front. Brett stayed down, keeping his foot pressing the accelerator all the way. He had calculated that he must keep pushing for three seconds more if his plan was to work.

In those three seconds the second cop had also managed to empty his .357 revolver into the seemingly empty truck cab. At that moment Brett pulled his foot off the accelerator and pushed down on the brake. The truck slowed but the cop car kept going. The two vehicles separated. The police car rolled back, its back wheels ran out of ground, and it tipped over the cliff. Brett heard the howl of the second cop and then the crash of the car hitting bottom.

Immediately he was seated upright behind the wheel.

"Come on," he instructed Olivia. "I'll get you out of here by foot." His only reply was a strange bubbling behind the curtains. He pushed the cloth aside to see Olivia in the sardine-shaped space sitting up with her hands stretched out toward him imploringly. The bubbling was made by the blood that was dribbling out of her mouth. Dotting her entire upper torso were shotgun pellet wounds. They had spun past the curtain and drilled into her skin—not deep enough to kill but enough to cause intense pain.

But those wounds did not decide her fate. Even carried by Brett, she would survive those. What she couldn't survive was the wound made by the .357 bullet which had drilled into her torso, just above her pelvis. It had probably torn away part of her stomach, most of her intestines, and destroyed her spleen. There was a halo of crimson on the back wall behind her body.

Brett blinked. For some reason she had not gotten down when he told her to. She had remained sitting up, perhaps to hold onto the sides of the enclosure better. Her surprise at being shot when she thought she was safe had kept her alive this long. Her adrenalin was pumping faster and faster as the realization of her own mortality grew. In her last seconds she was realizing that she would die horribly and much too young. Her awful panic was devastating to witness. Brett would not let her die that way.

He reached out and instantly put her into a calming sleep. Then, before the bullet could do it, he ended her life.

Brett turned from the curtain, a lump in his throat. A ninja did not feel pain, but he could feel loss. A ninja was all the more mighty for his reverence of human life.

But he did not consider Olivia's killers as human. He would only revere their deaths. Brett quickly dove out of the smashed front windshield, fell headfirst to the ground, rolled and came up walking toward the curved ledge. He looked down to see the cop car some forty feet down on its back. But even in the blue gloom he saw that the second cop, the one who had inadvertently shot the girl, was still alive and crawling from the wreckage.

Brett was already running backwards from the sight. He pushed himself off the ground, spun in midair, grabbed onto the upper frame of the truck's windshield and swung back into the driver's seat. Even as he landed, he was twisting the engine into roaring life. He opened the driver's door as he sent the rig barreling toward the curving ledge. Just as the front wheels left the ground, Brett stepped out of the cab and nonchalantly closed the door. He stood, motionless, as the truck arced through the air, turned over onto its back, then slammed down on the cop car and the tiny little man halfway out of the side window with his arms out in fear. His expression just before the truck squashed him into the Virginia dirt satisfied Wallace. There was some justice.

He moved back as the two vehicles mingled and their fuel ignited. A fireball the length of the cliff billowed up into the night sky, spotlighting Brett's dark figure against the trees for a second. Then followed a raging fire and mounds of billowing black smoke. That illumination revealed no one to the eyes of the two cops who had radioed in and followed on foot. The ninja was part of the night once more.

Morning came to Tylerville. Looking from the sheriff's office and jail, the moon set on one side of the mountain and the sun rose from the other side. Sheriff Nick Sherman watched it come up from the barred front window of his office. His beady little black eyes looked out from under his heavy brow. He felt the red stubble on his chin, then turned back to the two officers who had witnessed the crash of the truck onto the other patrol car.

The first one stammered as Sherman concentrated his stare on him. "It . . . it must've been the nigger gal, Nick," he said.

"Yeah," said the other one, eager to please. "I mean, when the damn thing comes barreling down the road on us, we looked right through the windshield at the driver and didn't see nothin'!"

"That's right, Nick," said the first. "Who else could it be but the nigger gal? You know how they blend when they're not smilin'."

"Sheriff," Sherman said in a tone indicating danger.

"What, Nick?" asked the first officer.

"I'm the sheriff in this town," he growled. "You call me Sheriff."

"Sure, Ni . . . , uh, yes, sir."

Sherman came around his desk by the window and moved to the open door of his office. He looked at the jail. It was a clean, renovated place. The old lights had been taken out and replaced by fluorescents in the padded ceiling. All the walls were soundproofed. There were a couple of modern desks, some typewriters, some phones, and two cells for the overnight prisoners on display. To the right was a locked iron door. Behind that were four more cells where they kept the serious offenders.

Sherman turned back to the nervous cops. "Where did she get the truck?" he asked them.

Both men looked at each other but could find no answer on their respective faces. They knew they had to answer but they also knew the sheriff wouldn't like it.

The second man decided to take the bull by the horns. "Damned if we know, Sheriff," he said respectfully.

"We looked for the license plate . . . you know, to trace it, but there was all this dirt covering it."

"And after the crash, you know, we couldn't find it at all."

Sherman knew. He had visited the wreckage himself earlier that morning. Tyler had taken him on with the express understanding he control the town's security and he took the job seriously and executed it with relish. "Tell me what you saw again," he instructed solemnly.

The two men waited until their boss rounded his desk and sat down.

"Well," said the second officer, "we come running up the hill right after we radioed you."

"Just in time to see the truck go barreling toward the edge of the cliff there."

"Then it . . . it just went over."

Sherman looked up at them after examining his blotter top. "That's all?"

"Just the explosion and everything," the first one assured him.

Sherman wrapped his fingers together in a big fist and placed it in the center of the desk. "It doesn't make sense," he seethed. "This little girl blows away five of my best men, then has the guts to ram a car when cornered."

"Well, you know how these niggers can be, Sheriff," said the second one. "Like animals."

Sherman looked up at the man sharply. The second officer nearly reared back from the stare. Nick Sherman was not the kind of man anyone took lightly, unless they were eager to join a heavenly choir. The sheriff unraveled his fingers, made two fists, put the knuckles down on the desk top and slowly pushed himself to his feet. The two officers nearly stepped back. At six-four from the top of his crew cut red hair to the tips of his steel-capped boots, Sherman made a frightening picture. His face was pock-marked by acne scars and some other wounds that couldn't be blamed on pimples. His neck was thick and heavily muscled, with an Adam's apple almost as big as a mandarin orange and veins as thick as a garden hose. Beneath his freshly washed and ironed shirt were more of the same. He stared at the men with a look that would wither a plum into a prune.

Then he snorted. He looked down at his fists and smiled. The two men relaxed, not knowing he was laughing at them. He couldn't believe these guys had the gall to call anyone else animals, especially an eighteen-year-old black girl who had the guts to fight back. He admired her strength, but it was an easy admiration. If she had still been alive he would have casually killed her, admiration not withstanding. "You sure she went down with the truck?" he asked.

"She had to, Sheriff," said the first.

"I didn't ask if you thought she did," he replied evenly. "I'm asking whether you're sure."

"Listen," said the second. "Just before the rig went over the edge, I saw the driver's door flap open, but nobody came out."

"You sure?"

"I'm sure, Sheriff," replied the second cop with assurance, "Nobody got out of that truck before it fell."

"And the boys are still going through the wreckage," added the first, "but they're pretty sure they've already found the girl's remains."

The sheriff thought about the evidence. He didn't like the way it felt, but he didn't see any other possible explanation. Initially it hadn't seemed likely that a pampered teenage model would have what it took to wipe out more than a half-dozen seasoned men, but remembering how hedonistically perverted they all had gotten after a couple of months in the town, it suddenly took on weight. The boys just hadn't taken the filly seriously and by the time she got her hands on the guns, it was too late.

"All right," said Sheriff Sherman. "Get out of here. Go back on duty." He didn't have to tell them not to let it happen again. The next time meant their automatic death.

The two officers left the office with such haste that they nearly got caught in the doorway. The sheriff waited until he heard the front door close before he sat down and picked up the phone. The connection was automatic. He gave his name and waited. Then he said, "Yes, sir. I think the case is closed. The problem has resolved itself and our borders are secure. Yes sir, I will strengthen our patrols at any rate. Yes sir, I understand. Thank you sir." He hung up the phone, the bile of disgust crawling up his throat. He swallowed it down.

Nick Sherman had never before called any man sir. He was always the leader, the boss. But Tyler had given him the power he wanted in a situation he'd be crazy to throw away. There was a certain pride in that Tylerville was a perfect evolutionary example of "only the strong survive." He had gotten this job in the time-tested way of killing his predecessor. And so far no one had been strong enough to usurp him. Again secure in his own superiority, Sherman opened his top desk drawer, pulled out some keys, and got up.

He walked through his empty jail lobby and went over to the metal door on the side wall. Utilizing three keys, he got the partition unlocked. He swung it open and stepped inside Tylerville's dungeon. It was a simple, but very effective box. It was reinforced concrete with no windows —only ducts in the ceiling to pump in air. Those same ducts could also pump in gas at any time as well as pump nothing at all—asphyxiating the occupants within hours. Those ducts were next to long lights located between the two cages on either side of the box. The cages were twelve feet tall.

Three of the cages were empty. In the last cage on the left was a small, huddled figure. Rosalind Cole sat in the empty cell on the floor against the back wall. Her hands were still cuffed behind her and that was the only thing she wore save for her own waist bracelet and her shoes. Sherman liked that effect. It was like she was a haughty little bitch who had been brought back to her true standing as a slave—just like the women in those science-fiction books about the planet of Gor.

The sheriff opened her cell and went in, already unbuckling his belt. Rosalind looked up, her eyes empty. She no longer had the strength to fight. It had been a long, humiliating night.

"Come on, baby," Sherman told her cruelly. "Get up for it. You know what I want. I told you how I like it."

Rosalind didn't move. She wouldn't give him the satisfaction of fighting this time.

"I told you I like it frisky, baby," Sherman said, "so come on."

Rosalind simply let her head sink so that her chin rested on her chest. Sherman angrily moved forward and grabbed her chin in one big hand. He wrenched her head up to look into his burning, insane eyes. "Look," he said with savage clarity. "You're gonna get it whether you fight or not, so you might as well make me happy. It'll be fast and painless or slow and excruciating. It's your choice. But you better enjoy it now, baby, because its the last you're ever going to get. When the man on the mountain gets through with you, you'll be lucky to have anything left."

Then the slaps and the little cries echoed through the empty, soundproofed box.

"I'm looking for a girl," said the sandy-haired man.

"Aren't we all?" the old man on the porch said with a cackle.

"You don't understand," said the young man reasonably. He was wearing a pair of non-designer jeans, some Timberline boots, and a tan long-sleeved shirt that was vaguely military in cut. "It's my girl friend. She was supposed to meet me in Richmond this morning, but she never showed up. I've been driving like crazy all over the routes she possibly could've taken."

The old man stopped rocking his antique chair and incongruously looked toward the center of town before replying. "Well," he said with a tense casualness, "she didn't . . . uh, couldn't of stayed around here. We don't have any hotel or anything. This is a quiet town, mister."

The sandy-haired man looked up the main street. There was a small green with a thin flagpole in the middle surrounded by low, ramshackle buildings. He saw a town hall and some other buildings that looked like a library, a diner, and a market, but all of them looked deserted. The only houses were two on the other side of town and the one he was standing in front of. Rising above everything to the left of the green was the small Tylerville mountain. The young man looked up at it before returning his attention to the old man.

It wasn't very big as mountains go, but it was richly covered by a sea of evergreens. The only jarring note amidst the jade blanket was the sudden glimpse of blue steel and gray stone that rose just above the top of the trees at the apex of the mount. It was the Tylerville School for Orphans.

"Well, maybe you saw her drive through. She had a 1980 Oldsmobile Cutlass Supreme, a pretty big, dark car with . . ."

He was interrupted by the screech of an old woman from inside the little house. "Joseph! You get in here right way! You hear me, Joseph? Don't waste yer whole morning gabbing to strangers." To others, it would have sounded like a normal complaint. But Brett Wallace did not miss the fear in the woman's voice.

"All right, dear," the old man immediately answered. He got up and headed for the door. But just before going inside, he turned back to the young man. "Son, your girl didn't stop in this town and if you know what's good for you, you'll look elsewhere."

"Joseph!" The old woman's shriek was unmistakably terrified this time. It's timbre nearly vibrated the dirty windows on the front porch. The old man turned quickly away and slipped inside.

Brett examined the house. It was falling apart. In addition to the windows which had not seen a speck of Windex in years, the clapboards had not seen a coat of Sherwin-

Williams for even longer. The structure just held together by the strength of its heritage, just like the town itself. The young man moved away from the place toward the center of town. He kept his feet pointed at the town green, but kept his head turned and his eyes pointed at the single house's porch.

Sure enough, the ragged curtain inside one of the windows was pulled slightly aside and he saw Joseph's face looking at him. As soon as Joseph saw Brett looking back, he hastily let the curtain fall back into place—but not before the young man was able to glimpse the old woman nervously barking into the kitchen wall phone.

Brett pulled his head back straight to look right at the town hall as he walked. He wasn't deliriously happy with his cover of Rosalind's boyfriend, but he had little choice in the matter. The previous evening's occurrences had shown him that he was dealing with a completely bought town. There was no real way he could've infiltrated the place quietly after last night. The whole place would've been suspicious of a stranger no matter what his alleged purposes were. So Brett had settled on a guise designed to be suspicious; not to be suspected. People wouldn't be doubting who he was, they would be wondering what to do about him.

And that was just fine with Brett. He'd let the danger come to him rather than go looking for it. As he neared the green, all his instincts told him that his reasoning was correct. In any other town, the green would be hopping. Children would be playing, people walking, and all the other examples of small town America at work. But in Tylerville, the street was empty. Brett was actually alone as he trotted up the steps of the town hall.

The doors of the supposedly public establishment were locked. Brett turned to survey the rest of the place from his vantage point. There were no shops, no restaurants, no movie theaters, no pharmacies, and no gas station. This place was not built for living in, Brett realized; it was designed for passing through. A lot of attention had been paid to making it the least attractive place possible. And even if there were an automotive or medical emergency, Tylerville made sure it didn't have the facilities to cope with it. The hapless stranger would have no choice but to move on. And if his car couldn't make it, Brett was sure the local constabulary would be happy to give him a lift out of town.

The police station, Brett saw, was one of the few places that seemed active. He considered going there to inquire, but he didn't want to enter the lion's den just yet. Instead he moved toward the second establishment across the way —a little storefront with the telltale sound of music coming from it and the smell of burgers wafting out a grinding fan on the side of the building.

Brett carefully studied the layout as he approached. A boarded-up store was to the left of it, while there was an alley to the right. Brett marched right up to the door, turned the knob and pushed it open. The sound of Delbert McClintock's "Givin' It Up for Your Love" assailed his ears and a heavy cloud of smoke assailed his eyes as he stepped inside. The only bright light in the place seemed to be following him in from outside. The interior was so completely covered that it was night all the time. Brett took in the details at a glance. There was a balsa-wood partition running the length of the establishment right in front of him. It separated the long bar on his right from the tables on his left. The partition was topped by colored plastic sheets which served as opaque windows. There was a three-foot space between the top of the plastic and the ceiling so the bartender could see the table patrons and vice versa.

On the back wall was a set of swinging doors to the kitchen and to the left of that was the jukebox pumping out the country and western tunes. The bar was an old one, running the length of the place along one wall with only bottles of booze and some "beer clocks" interrupting the view of the bricks. The beer clocks were those old-fashioned, plug in kind that had the name of the brew glowing behind the hands and numbers. The tables on the other side were square and supported by one big leg under the center, rather than four legs in the corners. The only thing out of the ordinary was a small upraised platform with the remnants of a musical band on it. There were some stands, a guitar, a harmonica, and a set of drums that looked unused since 1966.

"Close the door, would ya?" came an angry voice from the back of the table section. Brett came in all the way and closed the door. This bartender—a paunchy guy with a beard looked away from his conversation with a cop sitting at the bar in Brett's direction. Something that could have been a smile washed off his face when he realized that he didn't recognize Brett. The cop saw the expression on the barkeep's face and looked in Wallace's direction as well. His expression turned to one of concern also. Then the cop turned around, slipped off the bar stool, stalked over to the jukebox and pulled out the plug.

Delbert McClintock's voice wavered and ground out to a bass whisper as the voices of everyone else in the place rose. The cop stood in the back looking right at Brett while hooking his thumbs in his gunbelt. Everybody else got up but they were looking at the cop.

"What the fuck do you think you're doing, Cliff?" one of the other men raged, tromping over to the cop. The rager was also a big, ugly man, as were almost all the others. To a person, they all looked as if they had just escaped Alcatraz. The cop called Cliff didn't look at the angry man who was breathing heavy on the side of his face. He kept looking at Brett. Soon the angry man got the hint and looked in that direction. Then everyone looked over.

For a second, Brett was framed in everyone's eyes. Then Cliff came forward casually, smugly, his thumbs still hooked in his thick, fully loaded gun belt.

"Anything we can do for you, sport?" he drawled.

Everyone waited for Brett's answer. "I was just looking for someone, that's all," he said, making his voice assertive, but nervous at the same time.

"I don't know you," said Cliff. "Who are you looking for?"

"I'm just passing through," said Brett. "Looking for my girl friend."

The reaction was interesting. There was no sudden recognition, but a steady underlying understanding of the situation. Every man recognized Brett's plight, but they didn't respond to this specific instance. In other words, they were prepared for someone looking for a missing girl, but they did not immediately know who Brett was looking for.

"Well you can see there's no girls here!" the man who had yelled about the song said.

"Shut up, Sid," Cliff spat at him, then turned his head back to Brett. "What did she look like?"

Brett remembered the description Olivia had given him. "About five-seven, twenty-seven years old, black, loosely curled hair down to about her shoulders. Brown eyes, well built. Seen her?"

All the men in the bar looked at each other. "No," said Cliff. "I don't recall seeing anybody who fit that description."

"I saw a brunette lady go peeling through town," said Sid, gilding the lily. Some other guys in the place laughed at that. Cliff hurled him an angry look.

"What she look like?" Brett quickly inquired.

Sid was stuck a little there. "Oh," he mused, trying to come up with a good description. "I couldn't tell how tall she was 'cause she was sitting down, but she had that loosely curled hair you was talking about. I couldn't see much else, but she was pretty, I could tell you that. Nice eyes, pale skin. . . ."

"That wouldn't be Rosalind then," said Brett. "She's black."

It was as if he set off a stink bomb in the middle of the floor.

"Black?" Sid exploded. "You got a black girl?"

Before Cliff could do anything, the bartender put his two cents in as well. "She wouldn't be in here, mister. We don't serve niggers in here. And I think it would be a real good idea for you to get lost too."

The rest of the men agreed in a nasty mutter, moving

toward Brett almost as one. Only Cliff held back, his hand on the butt of his holstered gun, not sure what to do.

Brett stood his ground, carefully studying their faces. They were a pack of well-fed wolves, he decided. Their dislike of the Negro race was genuine. Brett had seen their sort of expressions before, at Ku Klux Klan rallies, at John Birch Society meetings, and Nazi marches. They had the look of narrow-eyed, narrow-minded sociopaths all made up with rage, smugness, and amorality. He didn't want to take them on, but he was ready to.

Just then the door behind him swung open and slammed against the wall. Brett looked over his shoulder at the same time everyone else did. Just behind him was a tall, craggy redheaded man in a perfectly tailored police uniform.

"Afternoon, Don," he said casually to the bartender. "How goes it today?"

"This . . . gentleman here," said Don, pointing at Brett, "is looking for a girl friend of his. A *Negro* lady."

"Oh, really?" said the redhead innocently, although Brett was sure the man was feigning the emotion. The big cop looked down at Brett. "Well, lucky that I happen to chance along then." He moved in front of the sandy-haired man and held out his hand. "I'm Sheriff Nick Sherman, Mr.—?"

Brett took the outstretched palm and made sure he shook just like a thin, thirty-five-year-old city slicker would. Firmly, but with no hint of the strength and control he possessed. In fact, he winced slightly for the sheriff's benefit when the big man returned the grip. "Craig," he replied. "Craig Miller."

"Well, come sit down, Mr. Miller," the sheriff charitably offered, waving his arm at an empty table in the middle of the floor near the upraised platform. "Can I get you a drink?"

"Nothing for me, thanks," Brett said gratefully, quickly heading for the table. "It's just that I'm a little worried about Rosalind." They sat down and the two went through the song and dance again about her description. But once again, Sid couldn't keep still when he heard about the color of the girl's skin.

"I tell you there's no way on God's green earth that girlie would stop here!" he yelled from the table he had been seated behind by Cliff.

"And even if she had," added Don, "there's no way she would have gotten much welcome."

"Come on boys," the sheriff said threateningly. "Take it easy."

"There's no way I woulda served her at any rate. . . ." Don muttered.

"Now just calm down everybody," Cliff soothed, looking straight at Sid from across the table. "Mr. Miller is obviously distraught. The least we could do is show him some Tylerville hospitality before he continues looking."

"He already said he don't want no drink!" Sid shouted.

"Would you shut up, Sid!" Sherman exploded, rearing back and swinging his arm in the man's direction. That quieted him down immediately, but the sheriff thought the scene was a little too intense to be entirely innocent. He tried to soften the edges a bit by commenting to Brett, "I declare, Mr. Miller, that boy only gets one day off a week from the Free School and he spends the whole time blowing off steam. He's had to spend the night in the tank more than once, I can tell you."

Brett leaned in conspiratorially, a look of honest concern on his face, "Listen, Sheriff, tell me honestly. Is it possible . . . I mean, has there ever been any problem in town with . . . you know, racial attacks?"

"Hell, no!" Sherman retorted.

"I mean," Brett rolled on quietly, "has there ever been a rape of a black girl in Tylerville?"

The sheriff calmed down quickly and approached Brett's question as the voice of reason. "Now I know what you're getting at Mr. Miller," he said plainly, "but I can assure you that there has been no trouble in this town that I don't know about. And as long as I'm sheriff, there won't be."

Brett mentally thanked the big man. That was all he

needed to know. Things were a lot worse in the town than he realistically suspected. But at least he wouldn't have to pick and choose his targets. Everybody was in on this one.

"Now, neither me nor any of my deputies have seen or reported seeing this girl friend of yours. She may have passed through but she sure didn't stop anywhere or we'd know it. So I suggest you get in your car and keep looking for her a little further down the road." As Sherman finished, he pushed his chair and stood; making it clear that as far as he was concerned, the matter was closed.

"Well, look, Sheriff, if you don't mind," Brett carefully began, "I think I'll just stay around for a little bit longer." The look on Sherman's face made Brett ladle it on a bit more. "I mean, it's about lunch time and its so hot and all . . . I think I'll just rest a bit before moving on. If its all the same to you.

It wasn't all the same to the sheriff. His face didn't soften at all. "This is a small, quiet town, Mr. Miller. We have lots to do with the Free School up on the mountain and all. We don't have time to do anything but look after our own. You just sit and relax a bit, fine. But remember, your girl hasn't been seen in this town. As soon as you're finished here, be on your way. We all have work to do. Understand?" Sherman looked meaningfully at Sid.

Brett's mind was smiling, but he kept his skin flaccid across his face. "I understand," he said slowly.

"Well, I don't!" Don shouted from behind the bar. "I already said I don't serve his kind in here!"

"For God's sake, Don!" Sherman shouted right back. "He's not a nigger himself! Give him a beer, for Christ's sake!"

"He's a nigger lover," Don complained.

"I said give him a beer," Sherman seethed. "On the house."

"Damn it, Nick. . . ." The bartender's voice trailed off as the big redhead stood his ground. Brett loved every second of it. It showed that the sheriff was not in complete control. They feared him, but they were too stupid to follow his orders without question.

Sherman stood motionless in the middle of the bar a while longer, then pulled on his hat and nodded at Cliff. "Come on, Deputy Potts," he said. "I want to talk to you. Outside."

The two cops left as Brett looked carefully over the other patrons in the place.

Outside Sherman marched halfway across the green with Cliff at his heels. He stopped under the flagpole.

"What is it, Sheriff?" the deputy asked intently.

"He's got a bee up his ass," the big man said quietly. "He's planning to do some more nosing around. I know that look. Keep him on ice until I can get in touch with the man on the mountain."

The sheriff looked up at the tattered American flag that blew in the hot wind. The sun was streaming through the little holes in the stars and stripes. It was the same flag that had been there since 1966.

"Discourage him," Sherman decided. "Damage him a little."

Chapter Four

"So you're messin' with a little black tail, are ya?"

Sid had come right over to Brett's table almost as soon as Deputy Potts had returned and sat down where he was before.

Brett looked over at the tightly muscled man with the face of a bony snake. He noticed tattoos up and down his arms. "Come on," he admonished. "Give me a break, will you?"

"No, listen, really," Sid said intensely, pulling a chair around and sitting on it backwards. He placed both arms on the top of the chairback and rested his chin on his wrists. "I've always been curious how a little brown poontang would taste. But every time I thought about trying it, it reminded me too much of shit." Then Sid laughed.

Brett considered kissing him. He considered it because his plan was going so well. Sid was obviously trying to pick a fight on Sherman's orders. That way they'd have a viable excuse to beat the crap out of him. The sheriff needed an excuse in case they decided to let Brett leave the town alive. It all depended on the next few minutes. Then it would be decided. Either they'd find it too great a risk to let him leave or not to. They couldn't afford him stirring up the mud but they couldn't afford to eliminate him if they thought some people would come looking for Craig Miller.

Only Brett Wallace wanted to shake them up. He wanted to get Sheriff Sherman and everybody above him so rattled that they'd make a move—a move the ninja master would be right on top of.

"What do you know about it?" Brett said to the chortling Sid. Meanwhile he was counting the bar patrons. Besides Don and Cliff there were four others. Sid had left Deputy Potts's table to Brett's left. There was another man beside the cop at that table and the cop had a gun. Don was behind the balsa wood and plastic partition and bar where he probably had a shotgun like his fellow barkeep, Stan. At the worst, he'd have one of those small, but extremely nasty sub-machine guns that Hama had warned him about. The first important thing he had to do was get rid of the gun carriers.

"Hey, nothing," Sid answered the question, throwing his hands up in mock innocence. "You're the expert nigger lover around here." Sid went back to his earnest listening position. "Come on, tell me, do they smell like shit? I mean, they look like they bathe in it."

There was one more table full of guys near the door, to Brett's right, playing cards. They had money on the table—lots of it. Brett couldn't see all their waistbands or pockets. He wasn't sure if any of them were armed. He'd know soon enough.

"Grow up, would you?" Brett told Sid's grinning mug. It didn't affect the man. He just kept on grinning. Then his expression changed to one of sudden discovery.

"Hey wait a minute, man!" he exclaimed. "I may have seen your nigger girl after all! I was walking around the woods last night when some sexy voice asked me if I wanted a blow job. . . ."

A small hum seemed to start in Brett's brain. He looked

86

at Sid and all the details of the man seemed to grow texture as if a flat film was suddenly shown in 3-D. The entire room took on a new dimension in Brett's mind.

"She smelled like greasy fried chicken," Sid went on, "but I never look a gift whore in the mouth. I may shove something in it, but I never look in it. . . ."

Brett seemed to feel a different pressure on the back of his head for every item behind him which he couldn't see. Without looking, he knew exactly where the drums were, exactly how high the platform was, exactly where the tripods were, and exactly how everything else was placed. The doors to the kitchen seemed to be permanently affixed to the corner of his eyes. He was sure that if anyone else came in through them, he would know—even if his back was to them.

"So I said, sure, I'll take a blow job from anybody," Sid continued. "Well, sir, she got down on her knees and said that she'd do it to any white man she could find, even if he were some ugly asshole from the city. . . ."

Brett felt astonishingly calm. An inner peace pact had been made with death so he could accept it—whether it be his or someone else's. The scales were even. He knew that these men were evil. He didn't have to see it, he simply knew. Their very existence displayed evil as clearly as if they had slavering devils on their shoulders. Brett was totally, completely ready.

"I asked her if she knew you," Sid told Brett, "since she described you to a 'T,' but she couldn't answer because she was already sucking my—"

"Just shut your fucking mouth!" Brett interrupted with feigned passion. He did exactly what Sid expected him to do at first. He tried to push the man away by the right shoulder. His hand seemed to go straight for that target.

Sid had dealt with that kind of thing before. He would merely, as always, grab the wrist, twist and pull, then start pummeling the guy with his free hand. Then everybody else would join in and the stranger wouldn't stand a chance.

Instinctively his bony fingers clawed out for the city slicker's wrist. It was moving toward his shoulder.

Sid's subconscious was surprised when it registered that Brett's hand seemed to stop in midair, even though it seemed to be moving forward at the same time. The back of Sid's mind was also surprised that the seemingly, flaccid fingers of the stranger suddenly appeared granite hard and oddly curved. But this was all in Sid's subconscious. It happened too fast for Sid's conscious mind to grasp.

As if in one motion, Brett's hand changed direction halfway to Sid's shoulder, snaked under the man's reaching arm, then slammed up against his nose so fast that no one saw it move. All it looked like to the others was that both men reached forward at the same time and before either could reach anything, Sid was hurled completely out of his chair, blood spurting from a hole in the middle of his face where his nose had once been.

Sid did a backwards swan dive with his arms and legs in the exact same position they had been when siting down. Just before he landed head first, his arms and legs started to stretch out. Then he hit the wood floor with an ugly crack and tumbled against the balsa wood partition. A question mark made of blood hung in the air after him for a split second, then made a red line from the table to his corpse.

Everyone stared in shock at Sid. Then they moved their gazes to settle on the stranger. But he was no longer where they had left him.

In the seconds immediately after he killed Sid, Brett straightened his legs on either side of the chair and leaped backward onto the raised platform. Even before he landed, his hands were quickly unscrewing the winged nuts that held the two cymbals in their tripods. When his feet finally flattened on the platform, the nuts were off and one flat, golden Frisbee-shaped cymbal was in each hand.

As Don looked up, his hands jerked for the MAC 10 under his counter. Cliff started to rise, his hand trying to grip the .357 Python in his holster. Brett hurled both cymbals at the same time. His left hand was perpendicular to the floor, moving in an arc as if he were bringing his hand down to point at someone. His right hand was parallel to the floor, swinging in a vicious arc to his left.

The cymbal in his left hand went straight across the room and sliced through the top of Don's head as if it were a whirring saw in a lumberyard. It parted his hair, his skull, and his brain. The cymbal from Brett's right hand curved under the other one, went right toward the back wall and became Deputy Potts's new tongue. The shiny, still sharp steel went right between his teeth, broke the bones that attached the jaw to the rest of the skull, then cut through Cliff's spinal column as well.

The blood spun off the edge of the musical blade and splashed into the face of the third man at the table. Meanwhile, to Brett's right, one of the three men at the card table was rising, pulling something out of his waistband. Brett didn't wait to see what it was. His left hand was already lifting the cymbal tripod off the floor. His right hand was gripping it by the base at the same time. Brett saw the gun coming out of the waistband at the same moment he hurled the metal tripod like a spear.

There was a glint of colored light as the bar's clocks reflected off the hurtling missile, then the three legs of the tripod were protruding out of the third gunman's chest. The tip of the tripod was hanging out his back.

The third man at the deputy's table was diving for the kitchen doors. Even as the tripod was leaving his right hand, Brett was grabbing a microphone cord off its stand with his left. The heavy microphone on the end served as the weight for the makeshift *kyotetsu-shoge* which Brett spun and threw precisely. The cord wrapped around the fleeing man's neck, which Brett broke with a sharp pull.

The third man flopped down, his nerves still jerking his limbs spasmodically, as Brett leaped off the platform. He slammed the toe of his boot into the head of the second-to-the-last man, who had been jumping up after seeing his card partner get a tripod in the chest. Brett felt the man's spinal column spread out under his kick to the back of the head just before the man landed on the table with both feet.

The last man reached quickly down to grab the unused gun out of his lanced friend's waistband. He turned, pointing the automatic at Brett's stomach. Brett looked down at him motionless and impassionately. He watched the man's hand.

The man was pointing an Army .45 at him. Specifically, it was the Colt Government Model Mk IV/Series '70 with Accurizor barrel, fixed military sights, grip and thumb safeties, grooved trigger, and sandblasted walnut stocks. Its weight with seven .45 ACP rounds was thirty-nine ounces and its overall length was eight and three-eighths inches. All that information was important as Brett waited for the man to pull the trigger.

He saw the vein on the back of the man's hand start to shift. Brett kicked out so fast his leg didn't even seem to move. His toes tapped on a certain nerve just under the man's hand on his wrist. The arm bent and the barrel of the gun was suddenly nuzzling under the man's chin. Brett fell instantaneously onto one knee. He chopped down onto a certain nerve in the crook of the man's bent arm, just above the elbow. The man's forefinger couldn't help but jerk.

The last man blew his own brains out.

Nick Sherman heard the booming report of the big .45 automatic from across the green. "Christ!" he blurted to the two deputies who had been reporting to him that morning. "I told them to beat him up a little bit. Not shoot him!"

With long strides that the other men had to trot after to keep up, the sheriff stalked between his office and the bar and grill. He threw open the door to see a wading pool full of blood creeping across the floor and seven corpses still pumping crimson out of their missing noses, foreheads, chins, ears, mouths, chests, and necks. The only thing missing was the man who had called himself Craig Miller.

"Holy shit," breathed Nick Sherman.

Steven was plenty pissed. He had to leave his beautiful young blond and go scooting off into town on his daddy's instruction. His daddy didn't have to stop having his fun to order him around, but Steven had to leave Terri secured in her cell while he went to get the sheriff's ass out of a sling. Something about not risking the security of their corporate headquarters with the possibility of Terri's escape. Now how the hell did they think the weak little girl would escape? And where would she run to? All her friends were dead, she was miles away from her school and even further from her home, everyone in town was a guard or captor, all the phone lines went through the Free School switchboard, every road was blocked, and there were regular patrols throughout the woods. What could Terri Cunningham do against that?

But still Steven had to leave her behind. It wasn't fair. It just wasn't fair. He readjusted his tie and smoothed down his three-piece suit as the car pulled off the mountain road and turned onto the main street. Steven reached over and picked up his needleless syringe case. The car braked in front of the sheriff's office and the Tyler son waited until his three bodyguards checked the area.

The three big, blond men spread out and scanned the town. Their bright blue eyes took in every square foot like the lenses of finely crafted cameras. They looked at the buildings, between the buildings, on the roofs of the buildings, and into the trees behind the buildings. They used binoculars if they spied anything out of the ordinary. As usual, the streets were cleared and the doors closed and locked.

Then they made a shield around the door of the car, opened the door and let Steven out. One walked in front of Steven and the other two walked to the side, slightly in back of the Tyler heir. If anyone tried to attack or shoot him, they'd have to go through the three big blond bodyguards first. They were more careful than usual, since they knew about all the deaths.

As soon as Steven was inside, he took up that subject directly with Sheriff Sherman.

"Fourteen men!" he raged. "Fourteen! First the girl friend of this woman kills seven with a gun and a truck, then the boyfriend kills seven more with a rock band! Who the hell is this woman? Where did she come from? Who brought her here?"

Sherman took the verbal abuse, then snapped his fingers. "Dewey," he called.

"Who's this?" Steven inquired softly.

Sherman looked at the deputy. The deputy looked back at him with a helpless grin on his face. He was preparing himself for the inevitable. "Bill Dewey, sir," the deputy told the younger Tyler.

"And where did we get you?" the young man wanted to know.

"Folsom, sir," Dewey replied. "In ten to twenty for armed robbery, assault, abduction, attempt to commit rape, and attempted murder, sir. Got out on good behavior in three. Was referred to your employ sir."

Steven smiled at the deputy as he would to a particularly apt student. Then he looked at Sherman. "Spell it out for me, Sheriff."

"Took a hostage after robbing a bank, sir," Nick explained. "A bank teller . . . ."

"A real cute one," Dewey interjected pleasantly.

"Tried to rape her when they got to their hideout, was interrupted by the cops, then tried to kill her."

"Was interrupted by the cops again," said Dewey.

Tyler looked at the deputy with admiration. "I'm surprised they let you out," he said.

"A few of my friends convinced the chick that it wasn't worth testifying against me," Dewey answered. "They're working for you now too."

Steven nodded. "I'm happy to see we are utilizing such help of high quality."

"Thank you, sir," said Sherman. "Knowing you would appreciate such a discerning eye, I made Deputy Dewey the officer in charge of procurement. He was the one who located and isolated the four other women for you, sir."

"Good," said Steven. "Very good. What happened this time, Dewey?"

"Damned if I know," he replied. One of the blond bodyguards smacked him on the side of the head. Dewey stumbled and nearly fell over. Then he started to come back with blind rage in his eyes. Sherman stopped him and whispered in his ear. Dewey calmed and nodded. "Oh, yeah, sorry. Damned if I know, *sir*." Steven just stood and watched the entire time.

"It wasn't until Deputy Dewey stopped the Olds that he saw it was two black women, sir," said the sheriff, "but then they were so exotic and so vulnerable that he thought you might like to take a look at them. He was in the process of testing one when the other got away. He could not interrupt the test so he sent Deputy Andy Post after the girl."

"How was she?" Steven demanded of Dewey, his eyes glowing.

"Great, really great," the deputy assured him. "Sir."

"Where is this girl?" Steven asked the sheriff.

"In one of the special cells."

"Have you questioned her yourself?"

Sherman paused. "In a limited capacity. You know your father's regulations concerning permanent physical damage at this stage of their preparation." The sheriff mentally snorted. He wondered what else they could call what they had been doing to the Tylerville women except permanent physical damage. In a perverted way, these girls were lucky Nathan and Steven Tyler had such a low success ratio. But then again, nothing couldn't be termed perverted when discussing Tylerville.

"Of course," Steven waved the mention of his father away. "Let us begin. I would see this black girl."

Sherman led the way as Dewey, Steven, and the three bodyguards followed him into the highly protected box attached to the main jail.

Rosalind Cole was outside the last cell, tightly lashed to the bars. Thin strips of leather and plastic-covered wire were wrapped around her ankles, calves, thighs, hips, waist, stomach, chest, neck, shoulders, elbows, wrists and all ten fingers. All were attached to the bars behind her. The men formed an audience in front of her as if examining a hunk of prime beef in a meat locker.

Steven snapped his fingers and one of the guards grabbed a handful of her hair and lifted her head for the young man's perusal. She had been washed and then very carefully, very expertly made up. Lipstick, rouge, eye shadow, highlights—all had been carefully and lovingly applied by the sheriff after he had chloroformed her in anticipation of Steven's arrival. After a few months of supplying living Barbie dolls for the warped Tyler son, Nick knew exactly what would keep him in the family's good graces.

"I see," said Steven. "Very interesting." Rosalind moaned. "She's coming around," he continued. "Perfect timing." He opened the syringe case, checked the various fixtures and pumped the drug into her veins.

Rosalind's eyes opened wide but she stared straight through the men in front of her.

"What's her name?" Steven asked.

"Her identification says Rosalind Cole," Dewey informed him. 'She told me that she was a free-lance fashion editor and her girl friend was a model."

"Is that your real name?" Steven asked her. "Rosalind Cole?"

"Yessetha," she managed to slur through slack lips.

"You're a fashion editor and model?"

Rosalind closed her eyes, nodded, and smiled. This was the best she had felt for days. "Uh-hmm."

"Your friend . . . ?" Steven looked toward Dewey.

"She called her Olivia," the deputy filled in.

"Olivia," Steven went on, "what did she do?"

"Little cow," Rosalind smirked, rolling her head around on her neck. "Spoiled little bitch. Always complaining. Always worrying. Never wanted to get off her duff and do anything."

"What did she do?"

Rosalind giggled. "Made funny little poses and funny little faces for the camera. Shook her little bootie."

"Your boyfriend," Steven changed the subject. "Who is he?"

"Boy . . . friend?" Her misty eyes opened in confusion.

"Craig Miller," the sheriff interjected intently. "What is he? A Vietnam vet or something?"

"Craig . . . ?" Rosalind breathed. "No Craig. Doug. Doug a nice little photographer. Tony. A nice little lawyer. Arthur. A nice *big* waiter!" Rosalind laughed deeply. "Big waiter. Nice boy. Nice, nice boy."

"Craig Miller!" Steven demanded.

Rosalind pondered the name, her lips pouting and his eyes fuzzing out of focus. "Craig? Might have been a Craig once. Craig? Where are you, Craig?"

Unknown to anyone, Craig was outside in broad daylight. He was listening to the entire interrogation through the air duct on the roof. One of the bodyguards had looked right through him. He had merely taken his dark blue ninja uniform and turned it inside out where it was the color of sunshine. It wasn't as easy as blending in with the darkness, but becoming one with the light was also possible. Brett Wallace had done it.

He had run to the hole he had dug in the forest for his ninja material, switched clothes, and run back again between the time Sherman had discovered his latest carnage and the time Steven arrived. He had stood against the side of the jail until the Tyler son had gone inside, then climbed up the side of the building without a rope to listen at the gratings. The building was constructed out of coarse concrete blocks so the scaling was relatively easy for him.

Brett didn't see Steven become angry with the lack of solid information, but he gathered something had happened when he heard Rosalind's slurred words get cut off suddenly. Steven had taken the expensive handkerchief out of his jacket pocket, grabbed the back of the girl's head, and stuffed it in her mouth. She hummed and hacked against it.

"She's a slut," Steven decided. "Where are her clothes?" Sherman ran out into the lobby, into his office, unlocked a file drawer and pulled out what the girl had been wearing. He ran back to Steven and handed the pile over. The young man tore through the material looking for some sort of clue, but was only left with her panty hose in his hand. Angrily, he wrapped the nylons around her head and knotted it in her mouth so she couldn't spit the hanky out.

"Call my father," he told Sherman. "Tell him what's happened. Ask what you should do, I'm going home."

Brett stayed where he was by the duct, only hearing Steven and his trained blonds leave. He slithered over to a duct which fed into the sheriff's office to eavesdrop on the phone conversation.

"Yes sir, I know I informed you that the case was closed and I maintain that it is. The dead girl is not the problem. The live one is." Pause. "I cannot guarantee the sanctity of our borders." Pause. "I'm not being negative, I am being realistic." Pause. "Even if this Miller got by our patrols, there is nothing he can prove." Pause. "Yes sir, that was the same thing I was thinking, sir." Pause. "I agree with you completely, sir." Pause. "Yes, I know what is at stake." Pause. "Yes sir, tonight." Sherman hung the phone up.

He rose and exhaled deeply. It had been close. The old man on the mountain was close to deciding that the sheriff needed replacement. As it was, Tyler felt that the town could survive whatever trouble Miller might cause by making sure there was no Rosalind Cole to be found. And the foolproof way of doing that was to send her up to the Free School. Sheriff Sherman decided that he was too tense from the phone conversation. He decided he needed some relaxation.

He left his office and sent Dewey back to his patrol. Then he went back to the special cell section. The girl still stood bound to the iron bars, the handkerchief and hose still in her mouth. She was extremely beautiful, Sherman decided. Even for a Negro. Especially for a Negro. He decided to forgo his usual approach. He did what he considered an act of pity. He raped her lovingly.

"Enjoy it," he told her drug-addled mind. "Enjoy it. This is your last meal."

Brett Wallace sat cross-legged on the jail roof, staring at

the air duct through the slit in his ninja hood, his fists clenching and unclenching.

The truck arrived at the stroke of midnight, nine hours later. Brett had stood absolutely motionless for six of those hours against the side of the building. Several deputies had walked by without noticing him. But now, as the truck braked in front of the sheriff's office, Brett moved forward. He was wearing the reverse side of his uniform—the dark blue—and carrying a representative array of his special infiltration implements. He watched, unseen, as two rough looking men went inside the office and came out carrying a steamer trunk. They threw it in back of the flatbed vehicle, got in the cab and started to drive off.

Brett didn't want to even chance running out in front of the jail in case Sherman was watching from his office window. The cop might not see the camouflaged ninja, but Brett didn't want to risk anything now that he was so close and there was so much at stake. The red brake lights might delineate his body just enough to worry the seasoned criminal in cop's clothing.

The ninja raced around the back of the jail and came out running toward the truck from the other side. Even though the rig was picking up speed, Brett kept pace with it. Almost as soon as he had gotten alongside, he threw himself down and over. He sailed between the big rolling wheels and under the truck. He spun in midair then grabbed the undercarriage of the vehicle with the tenacity and strength of a six-foot spider. He hugged the bottom of the truck as if he were lying on its payload floor. He stayed stuck to the spot all the way up the mountain.

Brett took the time to assimilate the new information he had learned. The overall picture had broadened again. The names of the "educational assistants" taken from the departments of his legal operation were false. They only served as fronts for hardened hoods who were recruited after parole as Free School and Tylerville guards. Brett knew that Steven Tyler was using some of these men to kidnap women for his sick use, but what was Nathan Garrard Tyler using the orphans for?

Brett was hoping that he would find out by letting the truck carry him into the school, but Tyler's security was better than that. The truck slowed outside the place, the driver got out and identified himself, the payload was taken out and the rig was driven away. Brett cursed his luck. If he could have switched places with the girl, he would have chanced it, but it was impossible. He could have opened the trunk and gotten her out but what would he have done with her then?

The truck took a turn onto another road other than the one back to town. Brett couldn't wait to see where they were going. He dropped off the bottom, waited until the back wheels had cleared him then rolled to the right side of the road so the driver wouldn't see him in the rearview or side mirrors. Without slowing, he pushed himself into a crouch, did a silent backwards somersault, twisted so that he landed on his feet facing toward the school, then ran.

He rounded a corner and the Free School loomed up in the distance before him. It was a humbling and cunningly designed structure, seemingly made to frustrate anyone trying to get in or get out. First there was a stone wall of at least thirty feet surrounding the whole thing. Brett spent some minutes checking the entire blockade. It was built in a semicircle, ending on both sides with a sheer drop of at least five hundred feet. It was solid, save for three serrated metal doors that rolled down, like the storefront protections that are locked into place in many cities at night.

No guards were visible in front of these gates, but Brett was sure that at least a few were always stationed behind. He looked for a strong tree to shinny up for a better view. He was impressed to see that every tree that had a limb overhanging the wall was trimmed back with chainsaws. Tyler wasn't taking chances. Brett climbed to the top of a nearby tree anyway. From that vantage point he saw that the space between the gates on the other side of the wall were steep, flat inclines with absolutely no hiding places.

Behind the three gates were three roads, each dropping off on both sides to these inclines.

The roads met at another wall with one opening. This was a more traditional wrought-iron gate guarded by at least six armed men. Each carried a sub-machine gun and a holstered pistol. Beyond that was the school and corporate headquarters. Which was which Brett couldn't tell. It looked like a medieval fortress built right on top of an ultra-modern office building. The sides were tubular steel and black glass while the top was concrete, granite, marble, and other stone. In this section there were no windows.

Brett cursed Tyler's paranoia. He saw no way to get in without there being some alarm first. It was possible that he could reach the school without being killed, but he was certain that all the orphans, all the missing people and Rosalind would be dead before he could rescue them. Many things went through the ninja's mind, but none of them concerned failure. He had no intention of giving up. There was a key to every lock, a solution to every puzzle. Brett sat in the tree considering it.

He studied the Free School. He realized that it reminded him of a military headquarters in World War Two. He considered what he knew about Nathan Garrard Tyler. He pulled the images of Steven and his three blond bodyguards into his mind. He began to fit the pieces together. An hour and a half later he decided he had enough to go on. He might be able to get the innocents out alive and he was fairly sure he could assassinate their tormentor. He might even be able to get out himself.

He smiled mirthlessly and dropped out of the tree. He fell twenty feet and landed on his feet without a sound. He rolled forward and came up running. The night was wonderfully peaceful. It was his time. As he moved that special calm slipped over him again—the sense of accomplishment and direction. The back of Brett's mind couldn't help but empathize with so many of the magnificent men throughout history who found fulfillment and even joy on the battlefield.

There was a terrible art to be found in killing, but it

could be an art, nevertheless. The only solace of the assassin was knowing that he killed toward an honorable goal. Many nations had warped that goal toward its own corrupt ends, but Brett was a country unto himself. He was his own ninja nation and he saw his soul unashamed.

He reached the spot where he had buried his special material. It was the place where Olivia had died. He dug up everything, then sat down to meditate. Within hours, Brett vowed, either he or Tylerville would be dead. Then he rose and got to work.

The two deputies who had witnessed the destruction of the soda truck were back on border duty. They stood with the two men who had remained behind that night as well as two newcomers to the job. The border rookies had been taken off the forest patrol to replace the two men killed by the truck. Everybody, as usual, was bored out of their minds. Four of the men were congregated around the hood of one of the cars, swapping stories about their robberies, assaults, extortions, and other crimes.

"Pipe down, will you guys?" one of the veteran deputies said, leaning against the hood of his own patrol car. He was the first one who had been in the sheriff's office after the truck ramming.

"Fuck you, Jack," came a harsh voice from the other car.

"Yeah," the first cop immediately retorted, "that's about your speed, Rosetti. You want to come over here and do it?"

The Italian cop moved quickly forward, but two men intervened before a fight could start. "Come on, take it easy," the second cop witness suggested. "We're all a little tight tonight. Be cool, it'll be all right."

"Yeah," said another. "I think it's about time we have our three o'clock coffee break. Break out the thermoses, will you Frank?"

The fifth cop opened the trunk of one of the cars and hauled out some airline bags. He closed the lid and set the vinyl carry-ons on top. Zipping them open, he pulled out some wrapped sandwiches and coffee mugs.

"It's about time," said the first cop. "I'm starved." He reached across the top of his car to take a steaming cup of java and a plastic-wrapped turkey sandwich from his partner. The second cop balanced his own refreshments in one hand while opening his passenger's side door with the other. The first cop followed suit, opening the driver's door and getting in behind the wheel. The two men set all their food and drink out on various dashboard spots, then leaned back to enjoy themselves.

The other four cops watched them and grinned as they chewed and sipped, still leaning on another car. Rosetti munched on a ham and cheese sandwich and looked up at the mountain. It was ominously peaceful, as usual. The only sounds to come from the thick forest were those of birds and insects. Tylerville wasn't a very exciting place, the ex-con figured, but he was being paid a hell of a lot just to watch its borders.

He snapped out of his reverie when the second cop in the car banged his head on the side window. Rosetti looked over. The second cop's head was leaning against the glass, blocking the Italian's view of the first cop behind the wheel. Thinking about the first cop, Rosetti realized that he acted pretty stupidly before. That first cop had seniority on him and was much closer to the sheriff's ear. He could put a bad word in if Rosetti wasn't careful.

The Italian decided to try and patch things up. He pulled himself off the fender of his patrol car and wandered around to the first car's driver's side—the sandwich and coffee still taking up both his hands. He nonchalantly ambled over to the door and leaned up against it.

"Hey, listen," he told the man behind the wheel as he looked off down the road, "I was just being a little up-tight. No hard feelings, huh?"

The first cop remained silent. Playing hard to get, Rosetti thought. Really trying to make him squirm, the bastard.

"I mean, all these killings in town, you know," he tried again. "Really got me on edge, see."

The first cop still didn't reply. Rosetti was getting pissed all over again. "Come on, man," he complained, leaning down to look the first cop in the eye, "the least you could do is answer , . . ."

But now Rosetti saw that he hadn't replied because he couldn't. There was a jagged, bleeding hole in the very center of his ear. Rosetti looked beyond the first cop in shock to see a thick, short arrow protruding out of the side of the second cop's head.

The projectile had gone right through the first cop's ears and buried itself in the other man's skull. That was why he suddenly tapped the window.

Rosetti spun around, his coffee splashing out of its cup and onto his hand. He didn't feel that pain because another arrow immediately sunk into his chest. Rosetti actually watched the sharp point disappear under his clothes and felt it burrowing inside him. He felt as if his organs were in spasmodic motion all at once. Then he felt himself going to the bathroom both places at once. Then he didn't feel anything anymore.

All three men died without making a human sound. The other men smelled it before they saw it.

"All right!" said one of them, "who farted?"

Those were his last words. They heard a thump coming from the roof of the first car because Brett Wallace wanted them to hear it. He wanted them to glimpse their executioner.

They all looked up as one to see the dark shape and the *kyusen* in his hands. They just started to move as Brett brought them down. The first man stood his ground while reaching for his gun. The arrow went right into his left eye. The second man tried to dive across the hood of his car. Brett sunk two arrows into his back which looked like angel's wings. The man fell to the other side of the car, already dead. The third man bravely tried to reach Brett's ankles to pull him down. He almost made it when he felt the horrid sensation of an arrow entering the top of his head and moving down.

He slammed down on the roof of the first car just inches

from Brett's feet, then slid to the ground––a single wooden antenna coming out the top of his skull. He flopped onto the concrete and then the night was silent again.

The forest patrol moved through the wood with practiced indifference. All half-dozen men were positive they wouldn't find anything. They never did. With all the security in town and all the security up at the Free School, their exercise seemed like a royal, useless, pain in the ass. The only action they had seen during the last few months were rousting the college campers on Bill Dewey's instructions. Now, that had been fun. Blowing away the guys and humping the girls was a thrilling reminder of the great raping and pillaging past, but now it only served to make them hornier than before. Why couldn't they come upon some campers every night?

The six men, armed with shotguns and sub-machine guns, moved up the leafy incline toward a tree-covered bluff in a vaguely circular formation. It wasn't anything planned, it was just that some guys had stronger legs than the others. Two guys basically took the lead, two guys walked to the side and the last two straggled behind. With every step they heard the crunch of dead leaves under their boots.

The last man along the way looked down at the hill they were moving up. He saw a solid rug of foliage. He looked up and saw the moving backs of the hill and then the solid wash of a dark blue moonlit sky above the summit.

Then he saw a seventh shape rise up between the front man's back and the rear man's back. It was a human shape, looking like a man with his back to him, only he seemed to have a long tail rising above his head. As the last patrolman watched, the seventh shape reached up and grabbed the end of that tail. The last patrolman heard a dim sliding sound and then his fellow officers started falling over–– pieces of them flying up into the sky.

Brett had let the front men actually walk over him before he sprang up from his cover, his *katana* strapped to his back. Using the skill of *iaijutsu,* he whipped the samurai sword out of its black scabbard at lightning speed. The men behind him didn't even see the shining blade as he whirled it in a circle around his head.

The draw itself was the first cut. The sword came out of its sheath and tore across the back of the lead man's head. Half his neck was chopped away. Even as his chin was meeting his chest without him having to nod, the sword continued its swing right to completely hack off the head of the man to the side. The blade's only real obstruction was the man's spinal column and the *katana* went through that like a machete through a sugar cane. The man's head did not pop off, as it would if chopped by an ax. The blade simply went through so fast that the head was severed but remained on the neck. The body kept walking for two steps, seeming not fully aware it was dead. Then the limbs slackened, the body fell forward and the cranium fell off the neck stump.

The sword continued on its whirling path. It moved behind Brett, slicing through the eyes of one of the men in the rear. He hardly knew what happened. One second there was a sudden obstruction that grew into his path and the next second his eyesight was gone. Then he felt the liquid all over his face and the pain. He dropped his gun, gripped his destroyed face and stumbled back.

With one literally blinding move, Brett had killed three of the patrol men. But he didn't stop there. There were still three more dangerous men all around him, each armed with an automatic firearm. All three pivoted toward the shape in their midst. One was in front of Brett—he spun to face the way he had come, gun at the ready. Another was to Brett's left—he turned to face right, the barrel of his Uzi pointed right at the ninja. And the last man was behind Brett, also bringing his weapon up to bear.

Brett made a certain *saiminjutsu* move with his free hand. It was a hypnotic motion which convinced the three patrolmen that Brett was about to strike again. They were absolutely convinced that they had to react immediately or die horribly. All three pulled their triggers at once.

Brett simply fell and rolled to the left. The front and back men blew each other away, their bullets smashing into each other's chest. They fell back, guns still chattering, as Brett spun between them and under the 600 rounds per minute the side man's Uzi was pumping out. The side man became aware of the shape rising up between his gun and his torso just as Brett drove the samurai blade into the man's chest. The sword went between two ribs, up through the heart, and out the back between the man's shoulder blades.

Brett pushed the barking Uzi to the side as he stood and the side man fell. The last bullets rippled up the hill and disappeared into the night sky. All the chattering died and Brett was alone once more.

Bill Dewey was cruising the back roads just outside of town, whistling "Whistle While You Work." He had reason to be happy. He had survived the confrontation with Steven Tyler, got a new partner to replace that dumb Andy Post, and was doing what he did best; hunting beaver. It wasn't the same without Stan's Tavern, but it was close enough to keep Dewey happy.

He stopped whistling and started lecturing his new companion. "First thing you look for is the car," he said pleasantly. "If you've got a Pinto or a Maverick or something, you might luck out with a cute chick, but it's doubtful. A really beautiful girl usually gets what she wants some way or another, so if you see some sort of sports car—an MG or something—go after it. Even a Rabbit, go after it. Any of them fancy foreign jobbies, go, man go!"

"Next thing you gotta look out for are them little physical things that tell you what you're dealing with. You see long blond or red hair, go after it. But if its cut short and you're not sure what you're dealing with, look at the neck and upper arms. If the neck is long and lean, go. If the upper arms are slim with no fat hanging down off the bottom, go for it. You might still be dealing with a dog, but pull 'em over for a look. You can always tell 'em that their tail lights flickering or something."

"What do you do if she's a looker?" the new man asked anxiously.

"Get her out of the car," said Dewey, turning a corner. "Any way you can. Get the whole picture. As for some identification, ask them to come take a look at something on the car, anything. Once they're outside they can't go speeding away. Then you can practically handcuff 'em and do a body search before they start making a ruckus."

"What do you do then?" the rookie asked almost breathlessly.

"Down, boy," Dewey asked. "Down! You can't mess 'em up too much if that's what you're thinking. The boss likes 'em unmarked. That doesn't mean you can't taste them, it just means you can't bat 'em around. That's why you always should carry some handkerchiefs and some of those." He pointed to the glove compartment. The rookie opened it to see a few small rubber balls. "Closing their mouths isn't half as effective as prying them wide open," Dewey explained.

He rolled down his window and put his arm up. "But don't worry kid," he assured the rookie. "You stick with me and you'll get more than you can handle."

Dewey heard a strange whirring as if a big bug were flying by the car window, but then he heard a boom and had his hands full trying to keep the car on the road. He forgot all about the whirring as he fought the wheel which was bucking and twisting in his hands.

"What's happening?" the rookie yelled, grabbing onto his door and the windshield. "What's going on?"

"We had a blowout!" Dewey yelled back. "Hold on!" He wrenched the wheel from side to side as the car skidded down the road. The smell of burning rubber filled the car, the horizon dipped crazily, but then the car slowed and settled. A white cloud caught up with them and passed through before Dewey swore and pushed open his door. The rookie followed his example.

They saw the patrol car had sliced to the left side of the road. The front half was on the blacktop but the rear end was hanging over a shallow ditch between the road and the woods. Dewey swore some more and kicked the fender.

Then the two men walked to the back to see the right rear tire totally squashed.

"Aw, shit," said Dewey, kicking the tire rim. Then he put his hands on his hips and stared at the thing. They both stood for a few seconds staring. Then Dewey turned to the rookie. "Well, just don't stand there," he yelled. "Fix it!" Then he walked back to his side of the car and got behind the wheel. He closed the door and yelled, "Come on, come on, the sooner you put on the spare the sooner we can keep scouting!"

The rookie started swearing. But he did open the trunk and get out the tire tools. Dewey felt the car rising and heard the rookie unscrewing the bolts and throwing them into the hubcap. Then he heard the wheel come off. He heard the other wheel scrape on. He heard the other bolts squeak back into place. But he didn't feel the car lowering. He waited a bit longer. The car didn't go down. He looked in the rearview mirror. The trunk lid was still up, blocking his view.

"Hey, kid!" he called. "Having any trouble out there?" There was no answer. Dewey stopped being pissed and started getting a little concerned. Then he realized the rookie was putting him on. He was pissed himself for having to change the tire so he was playing dumb. Well, Dewey would show him. He'd come running back there with his gun drawn and ready. If the kid still wanted to have some fun at Dewey's expense, the deputy would show him how the .357 Magnum worked.

He unlatched his door, kicked it open, jumped out and ran for the back of the car. He stopped once he reached the trunk. The rookie's legs were protruding from behind the fender on the other side of the car. Play possum with me, would you, Dewey thought while aiming the revolver. He blasted a bullet between the rookie's outstretched legs. He was fully expecting the kid to leap up screaming. The legs didn't move. Dewey hastily stepped to the other side of the car.

The rookie's eyes were bulging out of his head staring right at Dewey. His hands were claw shaped, his fingers vainly trying to pull a guitar string out of his neck. His tongue was fully extended out of his twisted mouth, hanging down like a gargoyle's. The thin metal guitar string was sunk almost one third through the rookie's entire neck. He had been silently garroted while Dewey sat in the front seat.

Dewey spun around with the gun still in his hand. He saw nothing. But he heard an angry hissing and then the gun was no longer in his hand. It was falling to the road as his limb had a spasm from the pain which had jolted into his wrist. He looked down to see a thin band of steel protruding from his hand just below the thumb. It looked like a bronze triangle with its top tip imbedded in his wrist.

He grabbed at his wrist with his other hand and then heard words coming from nowhere.

"For Dierdre Peterson," said the voice. Then another bronze triangle thunked into the top of his other hand.

Dewey held the limb up in wonder, seeing that the triangle had gone all the way through his palm this time. The two-sided base was just behind his knuckles and the pointed tip was protruding from his palm.

"For Tanya Bauer," came the voice again followed by another hiss. Another triangle tore through his shirt into his right nipple. It didn't go deep enough to kill him, but it went deep enough to make him fall back against the rear bumper and jerk to the right in pain.

"For the students," said the voice and a triangle sliced open his left nipple. Dewey screamed in pain and tried to do something. He rocked from side to side against the trunk hood, seeing if he could pluck any of the blades out, but the ones in his hands prevented his fingers from gripping.

"For Olivia Drake," said the voice and a triangle went right into Dewey's navel.

The cop doubled over, his arms crossing and his whole body shaking. He was still pinioned against the rear of the car. His weight pushed the auto off the jack and the spare tire fell on the rookie's outstretched arm, crushing it with the weight of the axle attached to it. Dewey stumbled back, hit the rear bumper again, then began to slide slowly to the ground—gasping from the pain.

Halfway there he saw a blade in front of his nose. The blade started rising. It touched his nose and sliced through the skin like a laser going through paper. Dewey jerked up away from the blade. The blade kept rising. Dewey forced himself to keep rising in front of it. He somehow straightened his legs and rose to his full erect height. Only then did he see the figure before him.

It was a living shadow with eyes. The eyes bore into him as the silhouette of the arm held a samurai sword tip against his chin to keep him upright. The shadow stood motionless that way for a full five seconds to let Dewey comprehend his situation. Then the voice spoke to him for the last time from under the floating eyes.

"For Rosalind Cole."

The blade streaked down and Brett Wallace disemboweled Deputy Bill Dewey.

The man fell forward with his hands outstretched, driving the blades deeper into his body while his entrails poured out between his legs.

The ninja slipped the sword back into its scabbard on his back, rewound the *kyotetsu-shoge* he had used to slash the tire as the car went by, waited until Dewey stopped quivering, then walked slowly back into the woods.

Chapter Five

Sheriff Nick Sherman awoke in a cold sweat. He hadn't done that since the day before his stay of execution by the Governor. It was that feeling of impending death he sometimes got. Everybody got it, he figured. Every once in a while, usually late at night, you'd suddenly get the realization that you were going to die one day. It became crystal clear to you all of a sudden that someday, too soon, it was all going to end. That you'd fall into the black cloud and never wake up again.

And then it was like an electronic circle of lightning that chased its own tail but never quite caught up. Then, suddenly, on discovery of mortality, the bolt connected with its tail and gave you a jolt from your forehead to your toes. There was a sudden, absolutely hysterical state of panic. Some guys in the big house never came down from it. They'd just get jolt after jolt and practically kill themselves before the guards came to beat them down.

Sherman had always been able to control it though. It

just got to him that once in the pen facing the execution chamber and then again last night. The jolt came to him in a nightmare. Not one of those simple nightmares where you saw pictures and it told a story, but one of those truly awful nightmares which were only made up of shapes, colors and . . . feelings. Horrible, irrational feelings.

But Nick had woken up and Tylerville still stretched out all around him in warm, comforting sunshine. The air-conditioner was still running in his apartment above the jail, so the room was nice and cool. Even so, he was sweating. He rose naked from the bed and went to the chair where his clean uniform was spread out. He dressed while looking in the mirror.

His body was battered and sewn together in more places than a football and hockey player put together. His torso looked as big and scarred as the Frankenstein monster. He was a lot better looking though, even though his skin was coarse and pockmarked. The marks added to his cruel masculine attraction. On him they looked natural. Sherman felt the two-day-old stubble on his face and decided to shave before going downstairs. After all, the jail was empty again. His little chocolate kiss had been moved up to the Free School.

Halfway through his shave, Sherman realized that no one had reported in yet. Dropping his razor, he ran back into his bedroom and looked at the digital clock. It was nine-thirty in the morning—a full three hours after he was supposed to be awakened by the morning report. The sheriff ran over to the console-sized ham radio rig in the corner of the room. He pushed the chairs aside and worked the dials standing up.

After ten minutes of trying to raise somebody at the borders or on the patrols, Sherman realized that none of the walkie-talkies or patrol cars were responding. All he could hear across the ham wave band was static. Sherman jumped back from the ham system, ran across the room, jumped over the bed, and reached for the phone on the bedside table. His hand stopped just before touching it.

The nightmare came back to him. He thought about

death again. He decided not to make a call to the mountain until he was sure what was going on. He told himself that the reason for the radio blackout could be one of dozens of things. A tube could have died in his ham rig. Sunspots could be blocking the signals. It could be dozens of things.

The sheriff slowly buttoned his shirt as he approached the window. Looking out, he saw nothing unusual. If he had seen anything but the empty street, it would have been unusual. But, as always, the town seemed deserted. The only thing that moved was the tattered, forty-eight-star flag which flapped in the summer wind.

The sheriff took his gun belt off the headboard of his bed and strapped it on. He took his revolver out from under his pillow and opened the chamber. It was fully loaded with .357 caliber bullets. He clicked it shut, shoved it into the holster, and opened the door to the stairs. There were no windows in the wall along the staircase, so Sherman closed the apartment door behind him and walked down to the jail in the darkness.

The job was geting to him, he decided. Even with the occasional perk of a girl now and then, lording over Tylerville was a strain. If he wasn't struggling to keep all the ex-cons in cop's clothing in line, then he was hanging out aimlessly during long, boring days. There was nothing to do except look around and use the captives when you got them. Even with the incredible amount of money Tyler was giving him, the sheriff's job was driving him crazy.

The sheriff grabbed the doorknob automatically when he reached the bottom of the stairs. He could see the ribbon of morning light coming from under the door as he turned and pushed; the bright daylight blasted across him and into the hallway. He walked toward his office even before his vision had cleared from the glare. He sensed the brightness of the rays diminishing in his eyes halfway across the lobby.

That's when he noticed Craig Miller standing next to one of the lobby's desks.

Sherman stopped in surprise, thinking the man might be

some sort of vision brought on by his nightmare and the sun in his eyes. But after the sunspots disappeared, Miller—in his jeans, boots, and shirt—still remained.

"I've got proof, Sheriff," the sandy-haired man said loudly. "What do you think of that?"

The sheriff blinked and swallowed. "What do you mean?" he finally asked, hand inching for his gun.

"I spent all night in the woods around this town," Miller went on vindictively. "And what do you think I found?" The man continued before the cop could answer. "Her car, that's what! Her Olds Cutlass was right out in the woods under some brush. Now do you believe me, Sheriff? Rosalind was here! She is here, someplace."

Damn that Dewey, Sherman thought. He told the Folsom graduate to take Cole's car up to the mountain garage where they keep all the vehicles, but the deputy must have screwed up again. The sheriff only thanked his lucky stars that Miller came back to town rather than getting to some other lawman.

The sheriff pulled out his gun and pointed it at the smaller man. "Craig Miller," he said, trying to remember the words, "I hereby arrest you for the murders of seven men." That's about the way Nick remembered it.

Miller's face changed from an expression of intensity to one of surprise. "What? Are you kidding? Come on, Sheriff, we've got to find Rosalind."

For a second Nick considered the possibility that Sid, Don, and Clift might have done all that damage to themselves with Miller the man in the middle. It was possible that a difference of opinion led the three to fight amongst themselves rather than tackle Miller. Lord knows they were dumb enough to do it. Maybe Miller just slipped out through the kitchen while everyone was going crazy. But then Sherman remembered that he wasn't really arresting him for any murders. He was arresting him so that he wouldn't rock the Tylerville boat.

"Get your hands up," the sheriff said threateningly. "You heard me. You're under arrest."

Seemingly confused, the man he knew as Miller raised

his hands hesitantly. Sherman moved right over, spun the man around and pushed him toward one of the public cells. Brett's face was pressed right between two of the bars as Sherman thrust the gun into the back of his neck, kicked his legs apart, and dug into his own pocket for the cell keys.

"Come on," he growled. "Spread them. You know the routine. Hit the position." Sherman was surprised at himself. Without thinking, he was mimicking the cops at all his own arrests.

"What the hell are you doing, Sheriff?" his captive howled. "What's going on here? I'm not the one you want!"

"We'll see," said Sherman, ramming the key into the lock, twisting, then pulling the cell door open. He grabbed Miller's arm and pushed him in. "Get in there," he said, swinging the door closed with a clang. He twisted the key back to lock Miller in. The man stood in the middle of the cell, looking aghast. Sherman turned his back on him, ran to his office, and headed for the phone while slamming the cell door behind him.

That was why he didn't see Brett's expression change from surprise to bland enjoyment. Sherman was doing just what Wallace wanted him to do. The ninja's entire ploy was to secure the safety of Rosalind Cole so she'd be in one piece when rescued. With her "boyfriend" behind bars, there would be no reason to make her disappear. Now Wallace only hoped Nathan Tyler was indifferent enough to let her live and Steven Tyler was perverted enough to take her under his kinky wing. That would at least keep her breathing.

Now came the hard part. Brett had to play it by ear to see how he would handle the rest of it. He moved over and grabbed the bars. Even with his ninja-trained hearing, he couldn't pick up everything that was being said inside Sherman's closed office. He remained in that position until the sheriff came out, looking at him strangely.

"What is happening to me, Sheriff?" Wallace inquired stridently. "You can't do this! Rosalind might be dead. She could be in danger. We've got to do something!"

Sherman cautiously approached the cell, trying to look right through his prisoner to see if there was anything else besides blood and bones beneath his skin. "What are you?" the sheriff asked. "Some kind of Green Beret or something?"

"Sheriff," Brett said, pleadingly.

"What happened yesterday in the bar?" Sherman asked.

"Never mind that!" Wallace retorted. "What are you doing to me?"

The sheriff seemed actually confused. His tough, coarsened face seemed tired. He sat heavily on the edge of a lobby desk, looking right at Brett. "I've got to ask you some questions, Miller," he said wearily, putting his Magnum on the desk beside him. "You answer them or I'll kill you."

Brett made his face appear shocked. "Jesus!" he breathed.

"Yeah," Sherman drawled. "Now were you in Vietnam or anything?"

"No," Brett replied indignantly, but honestly.

"What happened in the bar?"

"Those guys gave me a hard time," Brett said quickly. "Sheriff, while we're here gabbing, God knows what is happening to Rosalind . . . !"

The sheriff picked up his gun and sent a bullet ricocheting off a bar to the left of Brett's face. Brett forced himself to leap back in feigned shock. "Answer the question!" Sherman roared, slamming the gun back onto the desk and rising.

"All right!" Brett shouted. "That Sid character came on a little strong then took a swing at me. All of a sudden the whole place broke out in a brawl. I just barely got out the back door."

"Okay," the sheriff accepted the explanation. "What did you do then?"

"I told you! I spent the whole time looking around the woods. I found Rosalind's car. She's around here somewhere, I tell you!"

Sherman closed his eyes and clenched his fists. Miller's story was just barely plausible. Still, the vision of the bar and its seven corpses swam into his brain. He had broken up a lot of fights between his deputies in the time he had been in Tylerville, but never had he mopped up seven devastated corpses. Especially the day after seven other corpses were supplied by a little black girl.

And the story about finding the car began to get blurry too. It didn't seem likely that this one man would find it before all the forest patrols did. And it also didn't hold water that he would find it and avoid being seen by those same patrols. But if Miller was lying, what was the truth? That he had killed the seven men in the bar? That he had wandered around all night without being seen? And then suddenly Sherman remembered that all the men of his patrol hadn't reported yet.

Sherman opened his eyes, scrambled for his gun, and backed away from the cell. He stopped against the wall of his office, noticing that he was alone in a sunshine-filled jail with a small, sandy-haired man behind bars, but he was still more frightened than he had ever been in his life.

"I've got to ask you," he said quickly. "He asked me to ask you. Are you German?"

The look of confusion washed off Miller's face. The man's whole body seemed to minutely change. Whoever he was, he wasn't Miller anymore. The sandy-haired stranger smiled. But instead of answering, he sat down on the cot in the cell and pulled the one wooden chair over to him. Magically a deck of cards appeared in his hands and he began to play solitaire using the seat of the chair as a table.

"Where did you get those?" Sherman asked in wonder.

"From the bar yesterday, " Brett answered calmly, his eyes not wavering from the cards. "Three of your men were playing with them. But in answer of your . . . or should I say his . . . question. No, I am not German."

The sheriff stared in awed confusion as the stranger in the cell slapped down one card after another. His dexterity was better than anyone's Sherman had seen in Vegas or Atlantic City.

"I can understand why you ask it though," Brett went on affably, not taking his attention off the cards. "If you were to discover that I had killed those men, Tyler couldn't bring himself to believe that anyone except a member of the Master Race was good enough to accomplish that feat." The cards kept going down, Brett placing them on different piles after a second of deliberation. "I suppose that means that no one will be coming down here or I won't be brought up there for interrogation," Brett went on absently.

"No," Sherman said almost in spite of himself. "They're too busy for any personal attention."

"Of course," said Brett pleasantly. "I should have known. After all, I'm not a beautiful girl, am I? Or an innocent orphan with no one to run to, am I?"

"No," the Sheriff said again. "Who are you?"

Brett kept slapping down the cards. In the same tone of different voice and without looking up, he said, "Can't you guess?"

The sheriff thought back over the occurrences of the last two days. He remembered when it all had started. Then his eyes widened and he pointed at the stranger.

"You're the truck!" Nick exclaimed.

Only then did Brett look up. His expression was warm, open, and friendly. "That's right," he agreed. "I'm the one who killed Stan, Mel, Andy, and all the others that first night. I'm the one who rammed them off the road. I'm the one who killed all the men in the bar yesterday. And I'm the one who killed every one of your men on their patrols last night."

Brett saw no more reason to hold back. He had been hoping to intrigue Nathan Tyler enough to have the man himself bring him up for questioning, but it was not to be. The elder Tyler was having too much fun with his orphans to be bothered. Even if Brett had been German the instructions would have been the same. "Take care of it yourself. Eliminate him." So there was no longer anything preventing Wallace from playing his "full hand." There was nothing holding him back anymore.

"Come, come, Sheriff," Brett told the stunned man. "We both have our jobs to do. My job is to kill you all . . . your job is to try and stop me."

Sheriff Nick Sherman was thunderstruck for a split

second. Then he raced around the lobby desks and pointed his .357 right at the stranger's head. He was pulling the trigger when the stranger's fingers moved and another playing card suddenly appeared in his hand. Then the hand blurred. Sherman was just about to pull the trigger when his fingers opened in what seemed a supernatural way and the revolver fell on the floor.

The sheriff felt the lancing pain before he looked down to see the playing card buried halfway into his gun hand. Out of the corner of his eye he saw the stranger move his arms. A cord seemed to fly right out of his sleeve and out between the cell bars. Sherman heard a whipping swoop and that same cord wrapped around his neck with a sudden constricting sting.

Brett pulled and the ninja cord snapped taut, hauling the sheriff through the air to slam head first between the iron bars. Brett met him on the other side of the obstruction and grabbed the man's big Adam's apple between his thumb and forefinger in a *yubijutsu* grip.

"I've seen a magician throw a playing card from the stage into the lap of a spectator in the second balcony," Brett hissed in the Sheriff's face. "And I've seen people tear open their skins with paper cuts. You take that kind of accuracy and speed and combine it with that cutting edge and you've got a paper knife, don't you?"

Sherman tried to pull back, but his neck seemed permanently attached to the end of the stranger's arm. The stranger didn't even move from his standing position just on the other side of the bars. He didn't even seem to be exerting any effort to hold the big red head in place.

"Now I have a question," the stranger said. "What's the second way out of the Free School?"

"I don't know!" the big man croaked, trying to get the fingers off his throat.

"Come on," pressed the stranger, still unmoving. "No megalomaniac ever gives himself only one exit! There's always another way out. What is it?"

Nick Sherman clawed at the bars, kicked the floor, and gasped for breath. The pain seemed to go right from his neck into his brain. "I tell you I don't know! Tyler never tells me anything like that! I just make sure nobody asks questions!"

"I'm asking just one last time," Brett said with sudden passion, exerting more pressure on the larynx bone. "Where's the back entrance?"

"I don't know, I don't know," Nick Sherman blubbered. "I don't know what he does up there. I've never been there. I just make sure nobody else goes there either."

Brett finally admitted to himself that the sheriff did not know. It was true. He only lorded over the town proper and had absolutely no jurisdiction on the other side of the stone wall. He really had no idea where the emergency exit was. But Brett suddenly remembered someone who might. He looked at the big Adam's apple between his two fingers. He remembered that the thing wasn't a round fruit at all, but a system of bones and cartilage called the "cricoid process."

He held on with that one hand and reached for the keys on Sherman's belt with the other. He suddenly remembered the exercise where he caught the walnuts with two fingers. "Enjoy it," he told the squirming cop. "Enjoy it. This is your last meal." Then he did to the cricoid what he did to the walnuts and pulled back. Brett was left alone in his cell with some keys in one hand and some skin and bones in the other.

Brett indifferently dropped the crushed white calcium tubes on the floor of the cell and wiped his bloody hand on the leg of his pants. Then he unlocked the door of the cell and walked across the lobby to the sheriff's office. He ignored the frenzied gurgling that rose up from the floor, but he kept checking the office files until it had stopped.

Finding nothing, he left.

Joseph Neumann slowly mounted the creaky stairs to his attic bedroom. His wife Martha was still puttering around in the kitchen, but he was already tired. It was time for his nap.

Lunch, as usual, had been abundant and delicious. When

you weren't allowed to do anything but eat and watch TV, it helped if you learned how to cook. Over the last fifteen years, Martha had gone from being a toast-burner to a Julia Child.

Joseph let his wife stay in the kitchen. If she wasn't cooking, then she was cleaning. He didn't mind. He knew it kept her mind off the town's trouble. She had become obsessed—a little addled—about the situation. But who wouldn't be? Thankfully, they had been sixty when it started and already set in their ways. The change itself hadn't been bad—they never went out much anyway—but the pressure was terrible.

"Don't ask questions." "Don't talk to strangers." "Report anyone." "Report any car." "Keep your mouths shut." It was awful. Joseph just couldn't help not caring anymore. He just ate his wife's good cooking, watched his game shows and soap operas, and slept.

He reached the top of the stairs, opened his door to the left of the landing and went inside. His room was bathed in murky golden light, since he had the shutters closed. But there was enough illumination to see that there was a man standing in the middle of his room. It was a man dressed all in black who leaned on a curved stick with a handle. It was a sandy-haired man with gray eyes. It was the man who had been looking for a girl.

"Do you want to die, old man?" asked the stranger.

Joseph Neumann thought about it. "Perhaps," he said. "What do you have in mind?"

Martha had been a problem. She had screeched and howled and cried until finally Joseph had to put her to bed. He calmed her down just enough so Brett was sure she wouldn't try to use the phone. Even if she climbed through the window to contact the Tylerville police—as ludicrous as that seemed—she wouldn't find any police to contact.

Joseph came back downstairs and sat down at the worn Formica table.

"She'll be all right," the old man assured Brett. "I told her it was just like back in 1932. I said we had been silent then because it was our country. I said we are old now and should not stay silent. What difference will it make? We will be gone soon anyway. Must innocents suffer because we are not strong enough to stand up?"

"How did she react?" Brett asked.

"She understood," Joseph said with a sigh. "But she didn't like it. You know how it is. If you don't see it yourself, you tell yourself it cannot be. You won't believe it." The old man's eyes misted. "Just like 1932. . . ." The old man started to cry, then pulled himself up short. He coughed, wiped his eyes on a crumpled paper towel, and looked out of the window.

"You must understand," he said. "Germany was our homeland. When it went to war, we naturally thought what we were doing was right. And even when our boys did not come home, we still thought the Fatherland was doing God's work."

"When did Tyler contact you?" Brett asked gently.

"Shortly after we moved to America after the war. We did all right and moved here. We got a letter from his company in 1963. They asked some questions about our town and I answered them. After all, he was a fellow countryman. Then he came here himself and asked some more questions. Two years later he visited us and said that if we did what he said he would see to it that we lived comfortably for the rest of our lives. And since the accident I hadn't been able to work, so. . . ."

"What accident?" Brett inquired with interest.

"I was a builder," Neumann explained. "I had just taken on a new helper who had come over from the old country. A fine, strapping blond boy. Well, one day on the job, I tripped and fell off a roof we were working on. I got a sudden pain in my leg and lost my balance. I broke my back. My assistant took over the business."

"I see," said Brett, who really did.

"Yes, so Tyler offered us a big new house up on the mountain, but we couldn't bear to leave our little house here. I built this one myself you know." Brett nodded, smiling. "Only now I think we should have taken the other one. Things got very bad when the new police came in."

"I sympathize," said Brett. He handled the talk with Oriental patience. He could not rush the man, no matter how urgent his situation was. He wanted to get inside the school before anyone could discover that the "new police" were no more. But he couldn't get in without the old man's information. "What do you think made Herr Tyler move here?" he asked.

"I think it was the caves," said Neumann. "When I told him about the caves, he got very excited, it seems to me."

"Caves?" Brett inquired innocently.

"Yes. There was a large mine built into the face of the other side of the mountain. It now runs all the way up to the Tyler building's foundation."

"I see," said Brett. "That is very interesting."

"That is all you need to know?" the old man asked perceptively.

"I think so," said Brett, rising. "Unless you know any of the specifics concerning the actual construction of the school."

"Oh, no. I never went up there. It wasn't allowed. I just saw that they were using the best possible materials in the trucks that went by. It took them years and years to build the entire thing."

"I'm sure," Brett said, pushing the chair back under the kitchen table. He paused, his hands still on the back of the chair. "You might consider leaving town for a while."

Joseph laughed. "Where could we go? Remember, we have stayed here since Tylerville was created. Would we leave because it is destroyed?"

"Very well, then," said Brett. "I didn't think you'd go, but I thought I'd ask."

"Don't worry," the old man assured him. "And don't worry about Martha. I'm sure she won't try to call them."

"So am I," said Brett with a smile. Then he left. As soon as he got outside and into one of the Tylerville patrol cars, he reached into his shirt and pulled out a small round disk. He hadn't wanted to put the old man off by ripping the telephone out of the wall or cutting the wires, so he took the opportunity when he was bringing his wife upstairs to take out the phone's mouth mechanism. All he had to do was unscrew the bottom part of the receiver and drop the disk into his hand. After screwing back the bottom, the phone betrayed no sign of tampering. Now Mrs. Neumann could call whoever she wanted and screech as much as she liked. But no one would hear her.

Brett threw the mouth mechanism out of the patrol car window and sped toward the other side of the mountain.

To a ninja, all things are a ceremony. There is a ceremony to life, as there is a ceremony to death. Brett Wallace, the only American ninja master, was preparing to pierce the very heart of the enemy's territory. In the days of the ninja's genesis, the agents were hired mercenaries; sent to do dirty work noble samurai were unable to do because of their codes of honor. There were many cases, in fact, where the same samurai who hired a ninja to kill a lord would defend that same lord to the death. They gave their lives up to save face with the knowledge that the ninja would do the disreputable task that had to be done.

But Brett required more of himself. He was not a hireling. He commanded himself to right wrongs and save innocents from unjust fates. He could not infiltrate, kill only one man and then leave. His own code of honor demanded he see the entire evil operation wiped out.

And it was no longer a matter of a ninja fighting an enemy who held swords, staffs, and spears. The modern enemy possessed weapons that could spit out hundreds of deadly projectiles a minute. To fight them the traditional way would be like fighting sixty samurai per second. That was impossible.

What was not impossible, however, was defeating the modern enemy by updating traditional means. Brett, Hama, and Jeff, ever since his return to America, had been working on a ninja system which would be effective in the 1980s. This new system was not perfected, but it would be put to its acid test now.

Brett laid out the materials before him on the grass amid

the forest. He wore only a *fundoshi*, essentially a loincloth. Like a matador dressing for the main event, he carefully put all the pieces in place.

First the long, specially constructed *tazuna*, or long chest shield which strapped around his waist and neck. Then he slipped on the dark ninja pants. Over his calves he placed a specially constructed *waraji*—a section of armor which covered his leg from the knee to the ankle. Then went on the *yugake*—the ninja gloves into which Brett had installed special *shuko*, or, as they were more commonly known, brass knuckles.

Next went on the ninja shirt. Over both arms, the *kote:* hinged shields which protected the top part of those limbs. Inside special holders along the *kote* Brett placed special *shuriken* and *toniki*, which were straight throwing spikes. Over his chest he strapped on the *wakibiki* which was the Oriental version of a bulletproof vest. Only with the modern technology available, Brett had been able to make it capable of withstanding a .45 bullet at close range. Onto this he clipped smoke, flash, and stun grenades of his own design, which he had learned to create in his *yogenjutsu* classes.

Then went on the *uwa-obi*, which was an armor skirt, essentially, giving his legs freedom, but protecting his pelvis on all sides. Over this he placed a special sash. A sash loaded down with more *shuriken*, poison darts, his *kyotetsu-shoge*, and his *wakizashi*. On his back he placed his *katana*. Over his arms he carried throwing and climbing cords.

He was ready. His swords had been washed with a poison solution, as had all his blades. Unlike bullets, wherever the steel touched skin, the victim would die. The grenades, unlike the common wartime explosives, would stop his enemies at close range, but not harm himself. In a cave, in a room, in a hallway . . . although it seemed Brett's preparation was laughable compared to modern arms . . . . it was the foe armed with conventional modern weapons who would die.

The suit was thin, lightweight, and mobile. Brett felt no different had he been wearing a three-piece suit. He double-checked his location. According to the maps he had memorized before leaving San Francisco, the mine shaft was located some five miles from where he was. The ninja master moved into the brush, his armor making no more noise than a whisper.

That whisper was a chill promise. It was the sound of approaching death.

Chapter Six

Taylor Lockman was pissed when he saw the wisps of smoke rising from the brush on his video-screen console.

"Christ, Stew," he called to his partner, "look at this, would you?"

As the other man left the four screens he was studying, the wisps turned to puffs in front of the mine entrance. Stewart Barnes leaned over Taylor's shoulder and looked at the readout for camera number three. As he watched, more and more white clouds billowed up from the brush and rolled toward the videotape camera.

"What do you think it is?" Stew asked his partner. "A fire?"

"Hell, I don't know," Lockman moaned. "What if it is? What do we do then?"

"What we always do," Stew sighed. "Call in." Barnes picked up the phone that was attached to the side of the video console and pressed a button. A second later he pulled the receiver away from his ear and looked at it strangely. Then he hung up and went back to the number three monitor.

"Well?" said Lockman.

"Busy," said Barnes, not knowing Brett had left the sheriff's phone off the hook. "I guess we have to handle this one on our own." He looked at the screen as the thick white smoke completely engulfed the camera attached to the tree, obliterating any view of the mine entrance.

"I still say we should've called Bill on the ham radio," Taylor complained, holding the torch away from his head and trying to find decent footing on the rocky, sloping surface of the cavern.

"Deputy Dewey," said Barnes, utilizing their friend's title, "is definitely asleep. You know he cruises around all night. He doesn't like his work that much."

"Like hell," Lockman snorted. "It's just that there's a holy commandment forbidding any rape in broad daylight."

"It's called a directive," Barnes corrected his associate. "And the term for what Dewey's doing is procurement." Barnes had been thrown in the hoosegow for signing bad checks, but no one ever found out what he did with the money. That's because cops rarely try to locate missing hookers. In fact, they rarely knew about missing hookers. Barnes had gotten in trouble with some pimps though. But it was not the kind of trouble he couldn't handle. Especially since cops also didn't investigate pimps whose heads had been blown off very intently. But even though Barnes looked like something a vulture wouldn't even pick at, he took his new job seriously.

"Hey, Stew," said Lockman, the armed robbery man who had often gone on jobs with Dewey, "how come you didn't take the cop job down in the city?" Taylor heard his voice and footsteps echo down the dank cavern.

"What?" Barnes's voice echoed. "You fucking crazy? A guy could go fucking bonkers down there. Why didn't you?"

"Couldn't stand the uniforms," said Lockman. Then

they both laughed. Their laughter rolled away down the cave system.

They continued down the escape hatch, holding onto the torches and the special tube which had been installed along the left wall. They wanted to investigate this smoke as fast as possible, then get back to their posts. Since the sheriff had sounded the "all clear" that morning, the next shipment of orphans was going through as usual. And the two men wanted to see if there were any good ones when they got off the bus.

As far as they were concerned, all was right with Tyler-ville again. With Miller caught—and probably executed by now—and the black woman in the boss's clutches, every-thing was back to status quo. Their cameras looked into all the orphans' wards, they looked into all of Steven's cells, and they were posted outside of every Free School entrance, including the one in the rear. The cameras went everywhere—except Nathan's operation room.

The two men continued down the tunnel, knowing that just around the next turn was the cave which led to the entrance. It seemed to be getting a little lighter within the rock walls already. The pair hopped down the last little incline before the curve, then turned the corner together.

They stopped dead when their torches illuminated a weird sight. Standing in the middle of the tunnel facing them was what looked like a statue. A statue of a masked, armored warrior.

"Holy Jesus fucking mother of Christ!" Barnes yelled, nearly dropping his torch while clawing for his gun. He pulled it out of his holster and was about to pull the trigger when he noticed it wasn't moving. He blinked and lowered his gun a bit. The human-shaped thing was stock-still. It wasn't animate at all.

Lockman looked at the thing's head. It just seemed to be a solid hunk of black rock with no mouth or eyes and just a shape where the nose and nostrils should be. In the flickering gloom of the torch lights, they made an extremely macabre picture. Two T-shirted, jeaned ex-convicts and a royally appointed ancient warrior.

"Hell," said Taylor, "he looks a little like those space-men in 'Alien,' you know?"

"What are you talking about?" Barnes wheezed, his heart still pumping from the discovery.

"You know," his friend said, while using the cave wall for leverage, "that movie, 'Alien.' Those suits those space-men wore. This looks like it. Only not so bulky and there's no helmet."

"Would you shut the fuck up, you asshole," spat Barnes. "How the hell did it get here?"

"Jeez, I don't know!" said Lockman. "I don't even know what it is!"

Both men took their torches and moved toward the absolutely motionless statue side by side. They held their fire lights up and stared into the thing's face.

Suddenly two eyes stared back at them. They didn't have time to blink before Brett brought his *shukos* up into their chins. The brass knuckles shattered both jawbones and the men fell back. Before they had hit the rock floor, Brett had continued the motion of his upward punches to grab his *katana* handle in both hands and whip it out of its scabbard on his back.

As always the extraction of the blade was also the first cut. Brett swept it down and to the right to slice open Barnes's neck, then pivoted like a golfer to bring the samurai sword up through Lockman's back. The first man could not scream because his vocal cords were severed. Barnes watched his own blood shoot up toward the cave ceiling, momentarily surprised that blood could pump that high. Then his whole existence turned crimson, followed by black. Lockman open his mouth to scream, but some-where along the line, the message from his brain was lost. His entire body was too highly shocked by the nearly clean cut through half his torso. The yell died unborn as the man perished.

Brett quickly wiped the blade on the upper part of Lock-man's shirt. He replaced the blade in his scabbard, know-ing that the poison was still valid since he treated the inside of the scabbard with it, not the blade itself. Every time he returned the *katana* to its sheath, a new film of poison was reapplied.

The ninja ran deeper into the cave system, following the evidence of the two men's tracks and the strange tube that was attached to the wall. He kept running through the darkness until his senses told him that he was near the end of the cavern. There was a door covered by a thick black curtain. Brett stood by this partition for a few minutes, listening. When he was sure he heard nothing on the other side, he pushed the curtain aside and went through.

The tube, golden-colored and about six inches in diameter, ended at that point attached to the floor. In front of it and facing Brett was another heavy curtain. Brett repeated his listening technique. When he was sure no one was on the other side of this second barrier, he swept it aside as well.

The ninja emerged in a large, sumptuously decorated bedroom. It was almost baroque in its attention to detail and fine art accoutrements. There were rich Persian rugs on the floor, handsome original paintings on the walls, and a system of tubes on the ceiling. In some places along the tubes there were golden chains hanging down to the floor. In the center of the floor was a large, canopied, platform bed.

Brett assumed that this was the master bedroom. It didn't seem logical that Tyler would have an escape hatch in someone else's boudoir. Brett also felt fairly certain that he would have no security devices with which others could spy on him within these four walls either. Still he carefully approached the two main doors on the opposite wall.

Brett stopped for a third time by these door and listened. Ninja legend had it that a masterless mercenary from a ninja family was blinded at the age of seven. As he grew and continued training, his sense of hearing became so acute that he was even deadlier with his blade, which was disguised as a cane. Master Torii had told Brett stories of this remarkable assassin, who had wandered through the Orient under the guise of a masseur. Everywhere he went, his services were in demand since he seemed to fight by radar. He could pinpoint an enemy even through a wall.

The modern day ninja master heard activity through the wood of the bedroom doors. Logic told him that there would be guards by the master's chambers. His hearing told him where they were standing. Brett pulled out his *wakizashi* from his belt sash. He listened until he heard one of the guards lean up against the door.

"I can't wait until this new shipment of orphans arrive today," said the first guard.

"When are they supposed to show up?" asked the one leaning against the door.

"From what I hear, any minute," said the first.

The other man's eyes bulged in response.

"Yeah, any minute," repeated the first. He looked down the hall which turned off to the right. This particular section of the corporate headquarters looked like the hall of a fancy hotel. "I hope our relief gets here on time," the first muttered. "Fat chance," he decided and turned back to the wide-eyed leaner. "Tell you what. As soon as we go off duty, we'll go down to their wards and take a look. Okay?"

The leaner didn't reply.

"Okay?" the first guard repeated. Then he noticed that the man's wide open eyes were no longer looking at him. Then he realized that a stream of blood was oozing down the wall behind his leaning body. Then the door he wasn't leaning against swung open and a fast dark shape wrapped a cord around the first guard's neck before he could say another word.

The first guard gasped and choked, dropping his gun to try to rip the cord from his neck. But as much as he scratched at it, it didn't move. What did move was the shape holding the rope tight. He lifted the first guard bodily and ran toward the end of the hall.

Brett needed to see what was around the hall's corner and to be sure about it, he needed a shield until he saw that the coast was clear. Within seconds, he was rounding the corner, the choking guard in front of him. Twenty feet down the way were two white swinging doors with two more guards in front of them and two more who could be seen through the door's windows on the other side.

At first the men reacted in surprise to the sight of one of them standing on tiptoe with a rope around his neck. It was obvious these men hadn't seen anything more dangerous than a terrified orphan lately, which was all to Brett's advantage. But they were still hardened ex-cons so they reacted far faster than others might.

The first two men had their machine guns up before they realized that they had stars in their eyes. These stars were the five-pointed, poison-tipped *shurikens* Brett had immediately thrown from behind the cover of the choking guard's body. The next two men burst through the door and raised an alarm by firing. Their bullets stitched across the choking man's jerking body before Brett got two more *shuriken* out and tossed them with one hand. The men simply died on their feet. Their adrenalin was pumping so hard they hardly felt the blades go in, and the poison worked subtly. They simply fell over, without any spasms.

Brett raced forward, still holding up the bleeding corpse as a shield. He burst through the white doors and took in the scene immediately. He was at the end of the Free School structure which looked like a slab taken from a modern office building. The ceiling was very high, the space was completely open, and the floor was lined with two rows of occupied desks. To his right were one-way windows, which seemed black from the outside, and to his left was a long balcony overlooking the desks.

Spinning to face him from behind the desks were an even two dozen people who looked like young executives. On each desk was a computer link-up and television screen. Brett realized that this was the administrative section. These people were probably innocent of any wrongdoing. They were just the skeleton crew to take care of Tyler's legal work while the perverse and nefarious proceedings went on uninterrupted in the windowless structure above.

Across the way were two more swinging doors with four

more guards around it. Brett charged them, holding the bloody body in front of him still. He raced between the two rows of desks, moving unerringly across the stream of blood the choked guard was dripping. The effect this had on the executives was incredible. Suddenly the whole room was in an uproar, with three-piece-suited figures running every which way, and Brett burrowing through the mass led by a dead man.

The guards were criminals, but they still were unsure about shooting into a crowd of their boss's employees. But being the bastards they were, they were only unsure for a few seconds. Before the dead guard Brett had been carrying was fifteen feet from the second set of doors, the new guards had banded together and opened fire. Between their four Uzis, they were slamming out forty rounds per second, all of which were concentrated on the rag doll of a guard standing before them. The hurtling lead sent the dead man dancing back like a frenetic go-go girl of the sixties.

The figure stayed on dead feet for five seconds, then even the ammo couldn't keep him upright. He fell back, his entire front completely obliterated in a mass of pulpy red jelly. The man behind him was nowhere to be seen.

The four guards moved forward. And died. A grenade skittered from under a desk just as they got near the corpse. A sudden flash blinded them and then Brett streaked out from behind the desk. His *katana* was out of his scabbard and as his hand moved to the left chopped the first man's forehead in two. Brett brought it up against the next one's neck and kept twisting to the right until the blade opened a gash across the third man's arm. Holding the *katana* in one hand, he pulled out his short sword with his other and drove it into the fourth man's middle.

Both swords were out of the victims' flesh and back in their scabbards as Brett ran backward to the desk he had just hidden under. He had heard the sound of running feet coming from above him even before he had killed the last of the first-floor guards. Any second at least four more would appear on the overlooking balcony. Brett leaped sideways on top of the desk. Then he jumped again, this time soaring up twelve feet to land on the top of the banister running the length of the balcony.

His *kyotetsu-shoge* was unfurled and swinging even as the first man came through the balcony door. The two-sided blade ripped open his face. The man following him nearly had his arm chopped off just above the elbow. But this second man's bone had deflected the swirling blade just enough to save the third man from that fate. It didn't save him from the *toniki* Brett threw into his chest even before he started firing. The last man was confused by the jumble of hurtling bodies in the narrow doorway. He tried to push his way through only to trip, drop his gun, and slide to the edge of the balcony.

He stopped beneath Brett, his head hanging over the balcony's lip. The ninja heard another four guards slamming up the stairs toward the door on the other end of the balcony. Still standing perfectly balanced on the banister, Brett spun the weighted end of the *kyotetsu* with one hand while pulling out his *katana* and chopping off the fourth guard's head with his other.

The head dropped down to bounce off the desk below, then rolled to the black windows, spurting brains. The headless body made a crimson fountain that pumped pints of blood in a bubbling cascade. Then the next four guards arrived to the slaughter on the other side of the balcony—all the way down the high hall. They reared back as Brett hurled the *kyotetsu* cord at them. It moved so fast that they did not see where it landed. All they knew is that it had landed and they were still in one piece.

They charged forward as Brett jumped down from his perch. The quartet of new guards ran for his jumping off spot, pointed their guns blindly down toward the floor and started firing. What they didn't know was that Brett had thrown the weighted end of the *kyotetsu* so that it wrapped around the middle supporting leg of the banister. When he jumped, he had jumped for the cord, which swung him to the opposite end of the balcony—now *behind* the new guards.

Brett pulled himself up, vaulted over the banister and came up in back of the group. Not one of them ever saw him or knew how they had died. Brett had pulled out the samurai sword, hacked down the first, then the second, then the next, then the last. Hunks of these men bounced all over the tile balcony floor, literally waxing it with flesh and blood. Brett moved so quickly and so precisely that not one drop of the liquid fell on him.

He stood amid the carnage, his *katana* out, listening. He did not hear any more guards coming. Instead he heard the thrum of a bus engine. Brett looked out the tinged windows that rose in front of him across the room. He could see for miles around. He could spot a tiny stretch of tan which was the main street of Tylerville. He could see the huge wall that surrounded the Free School. He could see the three roads that led up to the main gate. He could see the courtyard in back of that gate. He could see twelve guards milling around that courtyard and the wrought iron gate itself.

And he could see the yellow school bus full of orphans coming up the road. He could see that the bus was full. That meant forty-eight people; forty-eight innocent people. There would be a guard for every four of them. There would be no way Brett could kill all the guards without harming at least one of the orphans. And if any of the parentless ones were so much as touched by any of his blades, the poison would work on them too.

It meant only one thing. Brett would have to kill the guards before they could get their hands on the bus. Brett instantly scooped up two of the fallen Uzis. He skipped across the pool of blood on the balcony, which was dripping over the edge like a red waterfall, and leaped back to the main floor. He landed on a desk, one Uzi in each hand. He jumped from that desk to another desk nearer the window. He stood and fired both Uzis point blank at one pane.

The roaring lead flattened, splattered, ricocheted, then finally dug into the plexiglass surface of the modern pane. Brett kept firing until both magazines were empty. He saw a patch in the glass that looked like a moldering swiss cheese. He looked back to the courtyard. No guard was looking in his direction. The place was soundproofed perfectly. The lead had not gone through the bullet-proof glass, but they had dug deep into the thick surface. That was the best Brett could hope for. He would have to do the rest.

Beneath the black glass was a little semicircular section of dense green bushes. It served as the courtyard's garden. Brett locked its position in his mind. Then he jumped off the desk, hit the floor, took one step and kicked out at the damaged section of the pane with both feet.

A four-foot-wide section of the glass was hurled outward. Brett had mastered the art of yell-less kung fu so the guards still didn't turn. They hadn't heard anything. Even the tinkle of the glass on the ground was prevented by the stuff falling into the garden. Brett was pleased. Surprise was still on his side. But he would have to move quickly and brutally. There was no place to hide in the courtyard. He would be completely exposed in the bright sunlight.

Brett came down on his feet inside the building after his kick. He immediately dove headfirst out of the opening he had made. He jumped down, spread his arms, somersaulted in midair, and landed on his feet. Again, the guards had not seen him. The last thing they were expecting was a hole to appear in the black glass and a black garbed man come jumping out, so no one was looking in that direction. They were all intent on the yellow bus that was getting nearer and nearer the gate. They began to move down the drive.

Brett killed the first three men without anyone noticing. These were the stragglers. They were a trio of guards who were coming laconically up behind the rest of the group. Brett pulled out the long sword and cut down the first, twisted his hand and swung back through the second, then let his momentum spin him all the way around to hack down the third. The fourth man noticed the ninja but that's all he did before Brett's blade had pierced his throat.

The sound of blood spurting alerted the others. Brett's mind assimilated their pattern. There were two right in front of him walking side by side. In his brain, they were numbers five and six. Behind those two was number seven. To seven's right was number eight.

Brett pulled his blade out of the fourth man's throat and tore it through the air to the left. The blade went right through the necks of both five and six, chopping off their heads. Brett let the momentum carry him all the way around and then he threw himself between the two headless corpses. He thrust his sword out in front of him with one hand, catching number seven right in the stomach, while pushing number six into number eight to deflect the man's aim.

The headless corpse fell on number eight's arms, knocking the chattering gun down, the bullets digging into the driveway. Brett pulled the *katana* out of number seven's stomach and twisted his wrist so the blade swung to the side. Then the ninja jabbed the point through number eight's eye and into the guard's brain. He pulled the sword tip out, still in a crouched position.

For a second Brett was camouflaged by a fountain of blood, pumping out from four places at once. Bodies went one way and limbs went another. Brett moved imperceptibly amid all this crimson confusion, effectively blocking himself from the four remaining guards' wrath.

Number nine was off to the left, bringing his gun to bear. Numbers ten and eleven were down the driveway a few steps, some seven feet away from each other. Number twelve was in front of them, positioned almost exactly in the middle of the courtyard.

Brett's right hand snapped the sword straight up. His left hand pulled a *toniki* from his belt and threw it into number nine's chest. Number nine's gun shot toward the sky as he fell backwards. Brett grabbed the samurai sword in both hands and screamed down on numbers ten and eleven, holding the *katana* above his head.

Numbers ten and eleven pivoted toward each other to get a bead on the seemingly crazy ninja who was running directly for number twelve. Instantly, numbers ten and eleven figured that they could kill the man before he was able to swing his sword at any one of them. They were so addled by the sight of a masked, armored man wiping out their fellows with a sword that they didn't realize where they were standing. The three guards made a triangle. Number twelve was the top point with numbers ten and eleven as the base points. Brett was running between the base points to get to the top.

Somehow Brett saw the trigger fingers of both ten and eleven as he neared them. He saw when they were both going to fire. Then he saw number twelve secure his machine gun against his waist. They were all going to shoot at the same time. Brett suddenly picked up speed. He went from being slightly in front of the two base guards to being right between them. The two men jerked reflexively to center their barrels on Brett's body.

They all pulled their triggers just as the ninja leaped. Brett threw himself up and then forward. One second numbers ten and eleven had a dark garbed target, the next moment they were shooting each other. Both fell back as number twelve shot at the open air. Brett was above him, twisting in midair so he looked like he was standing on his head seven feet off the ground.

As he passed over number twelve he threw his sword into the top of the man's head. Brett twisted again and landed on his feet facing the main gate as number twelve toppled backward, the hilt of a *katana* protruding out of his hair. The gate was opening when Brett remembered the six guards he had seen *outside* the wrought iron entrance. The bus had already reached them.

Brett didn't have time to retrieve his long sword. He ran down the remainder of the courtyard, pulling a stun grenade and a smoke grenade from his *wakibiki* as he went. He raced around the corner of the open gate just as the driver was opening the bus door so the first guard could get on. Brett leaped in the air again, landing on the hood of the bus. Another jump he was on the roof. Before any of the guards could react, he threw both grenades at the first guard.

They both detonated at the same time, the stun grenade crushing his chest and throwing him back while the smoke grenade engulfed them all in a grey cloud. At that moment, Brett pulled out his short sword and cleaved a long gash in the bus roof. He threw his sword back into its scabbard at lightning speed, pulled the gash wider, and dropped into the bus right between the front seats.

"Stay down!" Brett demanded of the orphans, his voice carrying almost as much power as his sword. This, too, was an Oriental art. It was the art of *Kiai*—which actually trained the ninja to use his voice as a weapon. It was a mystical art that Brett had not yet completely mastered, but he had the technique of it down well enough to glue the orphans to their seats with his order.

A guard tried to come up the steps of the bus out of the smoke. Brett buried the side of his foot in the man's face. A wet smacking sound echoed through the bus. The bus driver broke out of his shock to grab the emergency ax that was required on buses by law and swung it at the back of Brett's head. Brett felt it coming. He fell into a crouch under the blow, drove his elbow backward into the driver's crotch, then stood up sharply, driving the top of his head into the driver's jaw.

The first move rammed the man's balls out his rear end and the second move nearly tore his head off. The bus driver dove backward through the bus's side window. Brett caught the ax in midair after the driver dropped it. He immediately pivoted to the right and hurled the ax all the way down the aisle. It buried itself in the chest of another guard who was trying to climb in through the back door emergency exit.

Brett's hands came up again. In one was another flash bomb. In the other were four poison darts—each fanning out so that they looked like a lineup. Brett threw the grenade outside. A giant flash bulb exploded seeming to push the sun into everyone's eyes. Brett swung out of the bus door at the same time, his eyes closed. Before his feet touched ground, his eyes were open and he was already throwing the darts.

The first went into a guard's upper arm. Brett landed, stepped and threw the second into another man's back. The third took off from that position as well, landing in a guard's chest.

The last guard was trying to get in the back door even though his associate failed. Brett dropped, rolled under the bus, and threw the dart into the man's ankle. He kept rolling until he came out the other side of the bus. Then he leaped up through the side window the driver had broken through. He was just in time to see the last guard's eyes roll up as he fell onto the axed guard.

"Who can drive?" Brett called out. All the orphans who weren't trying to shut the bright light out of their eyes were too shocked by what had just occurred to answer. "Anyone who can drive this thing, stand up now!" Brett barked, reusing some of his *Kiai* training. Three stood up —a thin boy, a fat girl, and a well-muscled boy in the back.

Brett looked pointedly at the elder boy in the back. "I drove our orphanage bus back home a couple of times, sir," the kid said.

"Get up here and get this thing out of here," Brett instructed. "Go all the way down the mountain keeping to the main two lane road. Don't go off on any single lanes. Take a left at the bottom and go straight out of town without stopping for anything. Keep going until you get to Orange, Virginia which is seven miles down on route 37. Stop at the police station and tell them to get over here."

By the time Brett had finished his speech, the boy was seated behind the wheel and revving the engine. He looked at Brett's masked face with his questions showing plainly.

"Don't ask," said Brett. "Go!"

He swung out the door and closed it behind him before he landed. He watched the yellow school bus with the gashed ceiling barrel down the road toward the outer wall. Brett hadn't forgotten about that. He picked up one of the fallen Uzis and secured it in both hands.

A ninja is a master of death. To him everything is a weapon: be it an ice cube, a glass, or a playing card. So there was no reason that a machine built to kill would feel alien in a ninja's hand. Like everything else Brett had gripped, the Uzi suddenly became an extention of his body. He pointed this extention at the three guards who were standing in front of the metal gate.

Brett pulled the trigger three times. The men's heads snapped back one after another as if slapped. One after the other, they fell back against the metal and lay still. Brett pointed the Uzi one more time. He aimed at the red button inside the guard's shack next to the gate. He could see the button through the open door.

He pulled the trigger again. The lead served as a flying finger. It smashed the button into little pieces but it made the proper connection. The metal gate rolled up. Brett was pleased. The yellow bus kept rolling, even over the bodies of the fallen guards. Brett had successfully communicated the urgency across to the orphan boy.

Brett turned and moved back into the courtyard. There was no movement among the eighteen corpses he had made out here. Suddenly the ninja stopped. There was no movement, but not all was as he left it. He pinpointed the difference immediately. Number twelve was not in the same position that Brett had left him.

And one more thing. Brett's samurai sword was no longer imbedded in number twelve's head.

Chapter Seven

The Free School was a hollow husk. No more guards came charging at Brett as he effortlessly reentered the black glass from the hole he had made. The seventeen guards he had killed within were exactly as he had left them. They had no more blood left to pump out, but the red liquid seemed to be everywhere. Brett walked across it without slipping, but for a few yards he left crimson footprints in his wake.

He entered the inner sanctum of the school through the two swinging doors on the right side of the office hall. There he saw a wide tile hallway ending in two escalators and a stairway. On either side of the stairway, there were two more tubes reaching from the floor to the top of the steps. Brett listened as he walked. He heard no breathing from above. He was sure no guards waited for him in ambush. Most of the establishment's armed coterie must have been sent to escort the new shipment of orphans.

Brett took the staircase up in two leaps. He landed in

an attack stance just to be sure. He looked down a narrow stone hallway. The passage had flat, knobless metal doors on both sides. The hall turned off toward the right and there were three doors on each wall in this particular stretch.

Brett moved forward, feeling the emptiness of his *katana* scabbard. He approached the six doors by walking directly down the center of the hallway. There was absolutely no sound of his movement—not even the whisper of his armor. He passed the first door on his right. He saw that it was a classic dungeon door with a slit in the center to pass in trays of food and a barred, glassless window on top for the prisoner to look out. He saw all this without turning his head in that direction. He also saw this slit and window could be sealed but both were open.

Only his feet and eyes moved for a second. In the space of a step he saw that the five other dungeon openings were also unobstructed. Brett stopped. His fingers came together to make a solid band and they imperceptibly curved. The doors were staggered so none faced each other across the hall. First there was one to Brett's right, then one to his left and so on. Brett placed himself between the first and second doors.

Then he made a purposeful sound. He slapped his right foot on the floor like a sumo wrestler preparing to fight. The response was immediate. Men leaped up from the cell floors, shoving the barrels of their machine guns out the slit and looking through the open windows. They had not attacked prior to this because they had not heard Brett pass. They were too frightened to chance peeking out before he was in the midst of the trap, because they were afraid he might see them.

The hallway turned into a madhouse of flying lead. Brett was unconcerned. He had calculated the firing range the narrow slits allowed the men and he was already moving when they had shown themselves. He was flat against the wall to the left of the first door as the first man fired wildly. Brett just grabbed the gun barrel and wrenched it over so the bullets splattered into the door across the hall. Then he stuck his short sword through the slit, feeling it sink into an abdomen.

Immediately Brett fell to his face, his bloody *wakizashi* still in his hand, and propelled himself down the hall to the next door on his right. The man there was leaping all over his open gate, trying to see where the ninja was. The ninja was in the one place the man couldn't see; directly below him. But the gunman across the hall could see him. To kill them both, Brett executed an incredibly precise maneuver. With the last *shuriken* he had left in his right hand, he threw it across the way and punched up with his left glove.

The five-pointed star whirred across the hall, just sliding perfectly between the floor and the bottom of the cell door. There was hardly enough space there for a cockroach to crawl through, but the *shuriken* made it and imbedded itself in the gunman's toes through his boot. The poison did the rest. Brett's left hand shot out almost as fast as the *shuriken*, the brass knuckles slamming into the short machine gun barrel which the other gunman so kindly thrust all the way out into the hall. Brett literally bent the metal tube up between bullets.

The bullet before Brett's thrust went out into the hall. The bullet after slammed into the bent metal. But this gun kicked out five bullets a second. The second bullet hadn't broken through the bent barrel when the bullet after it slammed into it. And then the bullet after that. And then the bullet after that. And then the bullet after that. Now, the gun's hammer slammed down on the last shell which could fit in the ruined barrel. This ignited all the rounds remaining in the clip. The gun blew up in the gunman's hands. It had all happened in the space of a second, but Brett was already out of harm's way further down the hall.

He heard the rending smash of the metal weapon tearing itself apart and the scream of the man whose torso was ripped apart by it. He saw the man in the last doorway as he stood near the next to-the-last door. Neither man could bring their guns far enough around to hit him. He simply stood there, watching the bullets splatter into the wall.

With an enraged bellow, the man in the last door pulled the obstruction out of the way and charged out into the open so he could get a bead on the ninja. Brett threw his short sword like a *shuriken*. The blade sunk into the man's chest all the way to the hilt. The man fell back and shot the ceiling. The man directly beside Brett stopped firing when he saw the other go down. Then he saw Brett step right out in front of him.

The last man was sure that it was some sort of trick. He was so sure, in fact, that he didn't pull his trigger. A second later he realized his mistake. His mind told him that was exactly what the ninja wanted him to think so he would make a fatal pause. The last gunman stiffened in anticipation of the blade or spike which would sink into his body. A chill covered his entire body and he closed his eyes. Then he opened them again. He wasn't dead. He looked down at his body. There was no wound and no protruding blade. He looked up. The ninja was still standing right in front of him, his steel gray eyes on either side of the gun's barrel.

The last gunman hastily pulled the trigger. An empty click echoed through the hall. He had been so shaken by the ninja showing himself that he neglected to notice his bolt kick back on the last shell. His machine gun was empty. He looked into Brett's piercing eyes for a second, then fainted dead away. The ninja continued to the next hall, retrieving his *wakizashi* as he went.

Around the corner was a blank hallway with one door at the end. It was a solid doorway with a lock in the center. Brett took in everything as he approached it. There were no more security devices left in this section of the school. He moved his fingers as he walked and the lock-pick he had used to release Olivia reappeared in his hand. He listened as he slipped it into the lock.

He heard breathing. He heard three men breathing with deep, even breaths. He heard two more people sucking in air with great energy. He swung the door open and stepped in. All five people were waiting for him. It was a baroque scene. Brett stood in the entrance of a large, simple room. It was windowless and semicircular, as if built as a column on the outside end of the stone section of the school. It was lit by inset lights on the wall where torches would have been in medieval times. He stood calmly, facing the five other people in the room.

Three of them were the blond bodyguards. Each of them held a different esoteric weapon. The first had a small spiked club. It looked like a small baseball bat with steel triangular nails studding its crown. The second had a mace: a chain on a stick ending with a spike covered ball. The third had a claw on a stick: a wicked-looking half-circle blade which came to a bent-down point. If sunk into the skin, it would bite in and rip up, like a manual can opener.

Steven Tyler stood to the back of his bodyguards, holding Brett's samurai sword against the throat of Terri Cunningham.

"It's a very sharp blade," Steven commented. "So sharp that I cut myself while feeling it." Sure enough, Brett saw the thumb on young Tyler's other hand dropping little balls of blood onto Terri's naked chest. "It is so sharp, in fact," Steven went on, "that I don't think even you could get past my bodyguards before it sunk into this girl's neck. It would tear it open like a bazooka opening a book, don't you agree?"

Brett said nothing. He just stood and waited.

"Strip," Steven commanded.

Without pausing, Brett removed all his pieces of armor and his sash, laying them on the ground at his feet. He placed his *kyotetsu* and *wakizashi* there as well. He stood erect, wearing only his basic black ninja outfit.

"I said strip!" Steven screamed.

Brett gave in to the inevitable. He took off his hood, his shirt, shoes, and pants. He unbuckled the *tazuna* and put it down as well. He rose again, wearing only the *fundoshi*—the loincloth.

"All of it," Steven said with a smile.

Brett took off the last piece of clothing.

"So," said a triumphant Steven. "You're human after all. A little too human, I see. Too little." The bodyguards laughed. Brett stood, expressionless, as naked as Terri. Steven liked his victims completely vulnerable.

"We saw you out there," the younger Tyler informed him. "While you were busy on the bus, one of my friends kindly retrieved this sword of yours. It really is very nice. I'm going to enjoy using it." Steven's smile then disappeared and he nodded at the guards. The first blond stepped up and kicked Brett's neat pile of weapons and armor away from him. All the material scattered across the floor and bounced against the concrete walls.

Brett looked sadly at his ninja vestments, but he felt no shame. He had given them up as an act of honor. And besides, he wasn't captured. Not yet. He was merely using another life-saving device. He didn't want the girl to die—not after all she had been put through. He wanted to see her torturer punished.

"What's your name?" Steven demanded. "Your real one, not the load of shit you handed Sheriff Sherman."

"Brett Wallace," he answered flatly.

"Wallace, huh?" retorted the Tyler son. "And who the hell are you, Wallace?"

"I am no one," Brett answered truthfully.

Steven snorted. "Maybe not right away, but any second now." He indifferently motioned toward Brett with his head while looking at the three blond bodyguards. "Kill him."

The blond men came forward with their vicious weapons, eager to pound the shorter man into the stones. But they had made a bad mistake. They had left Brett his most powerful and effective weapon; himself. He stood motionless until the first man swung at him. The spiked bat seemed destined to collide with Brett's head, but then Brett's head was suddenly someplace else.

There were many parts of kung fu, or *Bujutsu* as it is more historically known. Two of these unarmed arts of

Bujutsu are judo and aikido. Both forms are effective, but both forms react to attack in different ways. In judo, when pushed, you pull. In aikido you turn. In judo, when pulled, you push. In aikido you enter.

Brett's head moved back and down as the spiked bat swung over him. The momentum pulled the swinging bodyguard to his left. Brett turned right and "entered." The entry was a vicious, singing swing of his arm up. His elbow stayed in one place. He just made his fist go from pointing in front of him to pointing up. As it reached its upright position, the knuckles smashed into the off balance bodyguard's face.

There was a crunching sound and the first big blond swung backwards, his feet completely off the floor, to fall into the second man with the mace. The third guard jumped forward, trying to bury his pickax-like claw into Brett's back. Brett leaped backwards and somersaulted over the blade which whirred by parallel to the floor. Brett landed to the left of the third swinger, who was bent all the way to his left, like a baseball player who had just finished his swing. Brett pushed his fist into the blond's kidney. The man stumbled forward, dropped the claw, and fell to his knees.

Brett heard the first two men leaping to their feet behind him. He threw himself backward, doing a handless cartwheel to land right in between them. They were all too close together for the blond men to do any swinging without damaging themselves, so Brett took advantage of the situation. He grabbed the hand that was holding the spiked bat in both hands while kicking up with his right foot. The side of his sole went deep into the mace-holder's neck while Brett bit into the spiked bat hand.

The mace man grunted and stumbled back, while the bat man howled and dropped his weapon. Brett returned to a standing posture and drove the heel of his right hand into the first guard's chin. Now this man fell back as well. It was time to put an end to this, Brett decided. He retrieved the fallen bat and spun in time to block the third man's claw which the blond had grabbed after shaking off his kidney wound. Brett swung under the blocked blade and drove his fingers into the third man's solar plexus. He pivoted and threw the spiked bat into the face of the mace man, who was coming back after surviving the kick to his neck. The bat bent his face back from the brow to his upper lip and he fell over for good this time, letting the mace go.

He had already began swinging the spiked ball when the bat hit him fully in the face so the weapon began to streak across the room where it would have smashed harmlessly into the wall. Brett grabbed the handle out of midair, spun, and sent it flying into the first man's head instead. The blond's skull cracked open like a red-spouting coconut as the heavy, triangular spikes dug into his bone and brain. The ball's weight carried him all the way to the wall, which he hit lifelessly and lay still.

The man with the claw came at Brett a third time, swung the blade overhead to come down through the ninja's face. Brett whirled and caught the blade. He actually caught it by slapping his hands together over his head. The two hands did not meet. The blade was caught between them. Even though the third bodyguard had put all his weight behind the blow, the claw stopped in midair. The blond looked in wonder at Brett's grip. His hands were flat against both sides of the blade without touching the edge. It seemed as if the guard could push the blade through the flat hands easily.

He tried. The blade wouldn't budge. He tried again, harder. The blade remained between Brett's palms without moving. The third bodyguard literally threw all his weight onto the blade's handle in a red-faced, neck-bulging effort to push the point just an inch into the ninja's head. It would not go.

Brett smiled beneath the blade and started kicking out. His first kick crushed the guard's right kneecap. The second kick shoved the guard's testicles into his intestines. The third kick ripped open his stomach. The fourth kick shattered his rib cage.

Before the guard could even feel the pain after the initial shock, he found himself back on his knees in front of Brett, blood pouring out of his nose and mouth. His hands were limp by his sides. Brett still had the claw between his palm up above his head. As the guard's vision dimmed, he saw Brett casually flip the blade in the air with a short jerk of his hands, catch the handle and swing down.

Brett left the claw buried in the third guard's head and turned to face Steven.

"Don't come near me!" the boy screamed. "I'll kill her! I swear!" He was so frightened that the samurai blade was already slashing the surface of the girl's neck.

Brett stood perfectly still except for raising his open left hand up to the level of his face. "I'm not moving from this spot," he told the Tyler boy.

His words did not soothe the terrified boy. "You've got to let me go! Let me walk out of here or I'll kill her!"

"No," said Brett easily, moving his fingers slightly so young Tyler could see them. "I won't let you go. You cannot go. I must destroy you."

"What?" Steven shouted. "What? You can't do that!"

"I will do it without moving from this spot," said Brett flatly, his left hand still up and open by his face.

"You can't!" Steven repeated hysterically. "You can't," he said a third time as if trying to convince himself.

"I can," Brett assured him.

"I'll kill her!" Steven poured out his ultimate threat with all the fear and rage that was left in him.

"No, you won't," said Brett in his regular speaking voice.

"Why not?" Steven screamed back wildly. "Because then I'll have no hostage? I don't care! I'll have the satisfaction of killing her! You won't save her!"

"Yes, I will," Brett reasonably disagreed. "You won't kill her because you can't. You can't because I still have one weapon more powerful than anything you possess. My mind. I can control you completely. You will try to push the blade into her throat, but it won't budge. Just like the claw your bodyguard tried to push into me, it won't move. It's like solid stone attached to your weak arm. It has a life of its own. It will float in space like a solid, unmovable bar. . . ."

Brett kept talking quickly, easily, mesmerizingly. Because that was what he was doing. He was using the art of suggestion and imagination—*saiminjutsu*—more commonly known as hypnosis. He was exerting his mental power over the morally weaker boy. What's more, the Tyler son knew he was weaker and that's what made the power work. Brett wasn't stopping him from killing the girl, he was stopping himself with his imagination, doubt, and guilt. Just as the Amazing Kreskin could make people act like chickens during his stage show, Brett Wallace was preventing Terri Cunningham's murder.

"You see?" he went on, "You cannot move the sword. Your arm is too weak. The blade is getting heavier and heavier. You can hardly keep it up. You see, it is already beginning to shake in your weak grasp."

Sure enough, the hand holding the sword began to vibrate. Steven looked at the sword in horror.

"You can no longer hold the sword," decreed Brett. "When I clap my hands, you must drop the sword as if it were burning hot. White hot. On the count of three I will clap my hands and the sword will burn your hand. One, two, three."

Steven looked at Brett, his mouth agape, the sword still shaking. The ninja clapped his hands. The boy suddenly stared wide-eyed at his own fist, then howled in surprise and pain. He dropped the sword.

The girl fell to the stone floor and crawled quickly away, her face twisted in silent crying. Steven hunched over, holding his "burned" hand by the wrist and staring at his unsinged palm. He looked up at Brett, then down at his hand, then up at Brett again. The ninja stood in the same place, his arms at his side. Steven was still sane enough to read the man's deadly look.

Without a word, Steven ran as fast as he could toward the door. It wasn't fast enough.

Five feet from the door, Steven heard whirring behind him. He grabbed the side of the door opening and jumped through. But before he could pull his hand away, he felt a sharp tug at his fingers. When he brought his hand back up, three of his digits were missing.

Steven had no time for anything but frenetic fear. He kept running. Brett came up behind him, spinning his *kyotetsushoge*. Halfway down the hall Brett cut off Steven's wounded hand with the two-edged blade. Steven kept running. As the boy turned the corner, Brett cut off his ear from ten feet behind. Steven kept running. Just passing the second cell door with the dead guards behind, Brett cut off Steven's other ear.

Steven spun, cried, and held his arms up in supplication. Brett cut off his five other fingers. As Steven turned back to run again, Brett cut off his nose.

Somehow, Steven kept running. His legs dragged him forward one tortured step at a time as his missing limbs left a red carpet for Brett to follow. All Steven heard was his own racked breathing and the whir of the spinning blade on the cord behind him. He subconsciously recognized when it was going to strike by the sudden catches in the whirling sound. He heard it again and his other hand was lopped off at the wrist.

Steven could go no further than the top of the escalator stairway. He struggled around to face the way he had come, just barely standing at the top of the up escalator. His tear-stained eyes looked out as Brett walked in front of him. They were separated by a distance of eight feet. Steven tried to mouth the word "mercy." With two quick spins, Brett chopped off both his arms.

The Tyler legs finally gave way. He fell all the way down the escalator, his head smashing open against the metal steps. Then the automatic stairs brought his corpse back up again where it lay, humping from the steady movement of the machine. But Brett wasn't there to admire his work. He was back in the large room, his pants, shoes and sash in place. He retrieved both his swords and put them in the sash. He left his shirt off.

Terri was huddled against the wall, still sobbing silently. Brett picked up his shirt and approached her. She tried to crawl away from him. He used accupressure to calm her.

"It will be all right," he said. "I'll bring you out of here, but there are things I don't want you to see." Brett tied his shirt around her eyes and picked her up. He carried her out of the room, past the dead men in the cells, past Steven's stump, down the stairs, past the office full of dead guards, down another flight of stairs, and out the main Free School doors and into the courtyard. He placed her among the foliage in the garden and took the blindfold off.

"Sleep," he said, using accupressure again. She closed her eyes and couldn't help but obey. Brett rose, looked behind him at the dead guards littering the driveway, then went back inside.

He found the operations room on the third and final floor of the building. He could hardly miss it. The cavernous room took up the entire third floor. It was filled with the latest and most expensive surgical supplies imaginable. There was operating table after operating table which were all empty, save one. On that lay the body of Rosalind Cole.

Next to her was a very old man in a wheelchair. Brett walked to within twenty feet of him before he spoke.

"That's far enough. You'll contaminate the patient."

Brett looked from the wizened ancient in the chair to the beautiful black woman. She wasn't breathing. The ninja was too late. The old man read his mind.

"Yes, she's dead," his thin voice crinkled in the vast room. "Medically speaking. But her brain is still alive. If you would allow me, I'd like to take advantage of that."

"No," said Brett.

"No?" the old man repeated as if he couldn't place the word. "No? Who are you, anyway?" Brett did not answer. Sudden realization flooded the old man's face. "I don't know you, so you must be Craig Miller!"

"I am no one," said Brett a final time.

The old man wouldn't let it bother him. "Well, welcome whoever you are. I am Nathan Garrard Tyler. Have you come to watch my experiments?"

"No," said Brett. "I'm here to stop them."

"Stop them?" the old man echoed, and then the words echoed in the hall. "Stop them? Whatever for? Young man, these are the most important experiments in the history of mankind. I am stretching the very limit of man's knowledge of his own body."

"Is that what you've been doing up here?" Brett asked. "Working on the live bodies of orphans and kidnap victims?"

"Only Negroes and Jews," Tyler explained as way of defense. "I started these experiments at Buchenwald and several other Fatherland establishments. I found the Jews to make better subjects than people." He laughed. "So I didn't want to affect my findings by switching races now."

Brett found himself shocked. It was a stunningly cunning situation. Tyler had opened the school and actually ran it straight for those of the right race. After the teaching was finished, Tyler's two rows of young executives would find the graduates' homes. That way no one knew that the Jewish children had disappeared. Everyone was happy thinking all the kids had found new homes. If Tyler hadn't raised a perverted son, the operation would have continued undiscovered for God knows how long. Even Brett's NEC computer hadn't picked up a whit of the actual evil that was going on here.

"This is a new set of experiments," Tyler rattled on, returning his attention to the dead black girl. "It is merely a supplemental investigation until I can continue my work with the new subjects I'll be getting soon." Absentmindedly, he picked up a scalpel and reached for the corpse's head.

"No!" Brett shouted, his hand on his *katana* handle.

"Now just stop this interference, young man!" Tyler flared, rearing back. "Steven!" he called. "Steven! Come here this instant!" There was no response. "Guards! Guards! Where *is* everyone?"

"They're all dead," said Brett.

Tyler took it in stride. He looked at the ninja for a second, then shrugged. "That's what comes of keeping only a skeleton security force up here. I didn't want to unduly frighten the other orphans or my employees. I thought it best to keep the majority of the men in the town."

"Where they could pick up any women who happened to pass by," Brett offered.

Even that didn't faze Tyler. He seemed to be well aware of his son's hobby. "Boys will be boys," he said as if discussing a lad who dipped a pigtail into a inkwell. Then he got wistful. "Women's lib made it so much easier. It made women think that they weren't victims, which of course they always were and always will be. The weaker sex. Humph. Now they're going all sorts of places by themselves without telling anyone. They're making it so easy."

Brett pulled his sword out. He had never met a more evil person. Tyler's casual assurance made his evil all the more cancerous.

"What are you doing?" Tyler demanded. "Put that blade away! You can't interfere with my experiments! It is absolutely vital that I continue." Tyler put one arm out to block Brett from the cadaver. "Most of the great scientific and medical advances of the twentieth century came from the Third Reich!" he lectured. "Where would the American defense and space program be if not for us Germans? I shall lead this country into the future with the most incredible discoveries yet. This I swear to you! Now, please. Leave me to my work."

Brett moved forward purposefully.

The old man hurled a scalpel into Brett's chest with a precision and strength that came as a total surprise. Only Brett's ninja instincts prevented his death. As soon as the blade bit through his skin, Brett had thrown himself back and hurled his free hand up. He knocked the speeding scalpel to the side before it could make any more than a flesh wound.

Brett fell on his back, cursing his stupidity. He had let the old man's age and seeming senility blind him to the truth. No man that evil was without an awareness of his own sick soul. Brett looked over to see the old man wheeling quickly toward a console. The ninja was on his feet as the Nazi hit the first button.

The floor fell out from under Brett. Tyler had pressed the trapdoor button where he disposed of his victim's remnants. Brett could smell the stench of death from below as he slammed his feet on the already opening section of floor. Brett remembered the exercise Master Torii had taught him. A narrow log was floating in the middle of a pool. Brett had to jump from the land onto the floating log and jump from it to the other side of the pool. Anyone landing on the log sank, but Torii showed him how to jump lightly and how to use everything as leverage. Torii merrily jumped back and forth from the log to the land.

Brett jumped off the swinging trapdoor the same way. Anyone else's weight would have carried them down, but Brett was up and out. He landed on the operating table, his feet on either side of Rosalind's motionless waist. He saw that Tyler was already completely across the room, hastily attaching his specially designed wheelchair to a tube that was attached to the wall.

So that's what all the tubes were, Brett realized. They served as a monorail for Tyler's chair. He could not run himself but he could travel anywhere by affixing a vise latch to the tube. Electromagnetic power controlled by some switches on the chair arm would bring him anywhere he liked.

"Good-bye," the old man called out. "You will never find me. I'll be more careful next time."

Brett jumped as he had never jumped before. The entire room swept by him in a blur as he concentrated all his energy on the little man in the wheelchair. As he flew, Brett saw a section of the wall swing out. The tube disappeared behind it. Brett was positive that it would take him through the caverns below to another means of transportation. If he didn't kill the man now, he *would* get away.

Brett pushed his body through the air. Just as it seemed certain he'd reach the Nazi in time, Tyler shifted in his chair and threw a whole handful of scalpels at Brett's falling figure.

The ninja wrenched himself away, spining his body madly to fall to the side. One scalpel stuck into his left arm as he went over Tyler's head and crashed into the wall.

Brett bounced off and slammed down to the floor as the Nazi shot by. Just before he got out and the wall closed behind him, Brett desperately slashed at him with his *katana,* but all his swings seemed to miss.

The wall slammed shut and Nathan Garrard Tyler was gone.

Brett Wallace rose slowly to his feet, his expression changing. He no longer looked angry, intent, unsure, and desperate. Those emotions seemed to drain completely from his face, leaving nothing but a blank shell. He plucked the scalpel out of his arm without looking at it. It too was just a flesh wound. He stood with his sword pointing at the floor for a second, listening to the silence.

He walked back to where the body of Rosalind Cole lay. He put his sword back in his sash and put his hands flat on the operating table. He looked into her peaceful, dead face and listened.

In back of the silence was a humming. It was the humming of Tyler's wheelchair as it streaked down through the dark caves. Brett looked at Rosalind and smiled with pity. All he could do now was pray that somehow she knew she had been avenged.

Neither Brett nor Tyler saw it. It was too dark in the caves to see. But Brett pictured in his mind the exercises he had done with Jeff Archer. With his sword he had peeled fruit thrown at him before it hit the ground. First a grapefruit, then an orange, then an apple, then a grape. He had cut away the skin without touching the meat.

Before Nathan Garrard Tyler had gotten fifty yards, his chest fell away from his guts. His shirt fell open and then every inch of skin from his shoulders to his penis fell off. All his internal organs fell out after.

Brett heard the scream all the way up in the operating room. He waited until the horrid, wrenching cries grew dim and died. Then he went outside to bring Terri Cunningham—and himself—back to sanity.

MEN OF ACTION BOOKS
NINJA MASTER
By Wade Barker

The Ninja Master is Brett Wallace, San Francisco partner in the hottest Japanese restaurant in town and a martial-arts studio. He marries a beautiful Japanese woman and begins to take over his father's real-estate business—when tragedy strikes. His pregnant wife and parents are savagely murdered by a hopped-up motorcycle gang—and the killers escape justice when their case is thrown out of court on a technicality.

Revenge becomes Wallace's career. He brings his own form of justice to the killers and then escapes to a secret Ninja camp in Japan to become a master in the deadly craft. Armed with a new identity, he roves the world bringing justice to people who have been wrongfully harmed and whom the legal system has failed. From slavers in South Africa to bizarre religious cults to the Chinese Mafia, the Ninja Master is feared and revered as he combines a talent for modern justice with an ancient art of killing.